MYRA DUFFY

SUSIE'S STORY

The companion novella to

The House at Ettrick Bay

www.myraduffywriter.com

Characters in this novella bear no relation to any persons living or dead. Any such resemblance is co-incidental.

Author's note

This is the story of how Susie Littlejohn came to inherit the house at Ettrick Bay. The story of what she decided to do with her inheritance is told in

The House at Ettrick Bay

THE ISLE OF BUTE SERIES

The House at Ettrick Bay

Last Ferry to Bute

Last Dance at the Rothesay Pavilion

Endgame at Port Bannatyne

Grave Matters at St Blane's

Death at the Kyles of Bute

PROLOGUE

The little girl skipped and hopped on the driveway. Faster and faster flew the ropes with a skill born of long practice. It was much more fun at school when there were others to play with, her best friends Doreen and Mary, one at each end to ply the ropes and count the steps, but she sang the songs anyway.

> 'Vote, vote, vote for dearest Susie,
> Who's that knocking at the door?
> If it's Mary let her in
> Then we'll sock her on the chin,
> And we won't want Susie any more.
> Shut the door.'

She stopped to catch her breath and gaze out through the trees over by the gate. If she stood on tiptoe, she could glimpse the golden sands and the waters of Ettrick Bay in the distance, far below.

'Lucky you,' Mary had said, 'going to Bute for the whole holiday. We might get a week at my cousin's caravan in Girvan, if no one else is there.'

Susie had been coming to the island every year for as long as she could remember and while it was agreeable here with her aunt and uncle, enjoying trips to the beach at Ettrick Bay or further afield into the town of Rothesay, sometimes she felt lonely. She missed the city, the bustle and the noise of Glasgow, and most of all she missed her mother.

'Robert and Jeanie are very kind to have you for the summer,' her mother reminded her as they made the journey from the quayside at the Broomielaw in Glasgow. Susie loved the trip on the giant paddle steamer and insisted on staying on deck whatever the weather, all the way down the Firth of Clyde, past the din of hammer on steel in the many shipyards, then out into the open water towards the calm of Rothesay Bay. Sometimes the boat was so crowded it listed to one side as they approached the pier, the passengers competing to be first to catch a glimpse of their eagerly anticipated holiday destination.

'Glasgow will be deserted,' said Susie's mother. 'Lots of people will be coming here for the two weeks of the Glasgow holiday, the 'Fair' as it's called.'

Susie frowned. 'Why?'

'Because,' was the reply, 'every year at this time the factories close for two weeks to allow the workers to have a break.'

Once off the steamer Susie and her mother hurried across the road to Guildford Square, eager to be first in the queue for the bus to Ettrick Bay. If she was lucky Susie managed to find a window seat where she would put her face right up against the glass as the bus headed first to Ardbeg, then through Port Bannatyne past the garden with the monkey puzzle tree, past the boats nestled for summer in the bay, before reaching the parade of shops.

The bus stopped opposite the quay to let some of the passengers off and when it started up again she began to name the shops quietly one by one: the café, the pub, the grocers, a second pub, another grocer's shop. Beside the Crown Hotel was the butcher's and at the end of the row, best of all, was her favourite ice cream shop.

On the far side of the village the bus passed the school, shuttered and silent, but the boatyard was busy with owners sprucing up their boats for the summer season. The bus made a sharp turn left at Kames Castle and when they reached the old ruined church at Croc-an-Rath Susie could hardly contain her excitement, knowing they were almost at their destination.

It wasn't an official stop, but the driver let them off at the smithy with a cheerful, 'Have a good holiday,' and they began the walk up the hill to where her aunt and uncle lived. She grasped her mother's hand more tightly as they tiptoed across the shaky bridge signposted Kilbride. Even in summer the burn below could gush and tumble down the hill in an alarming way.

'Thank goodness we sent your trunk on ahead,' her mother sighed as they at last reached the large metal gates standing at the entrance to the property. Fortunately there was a little side gate, much easier to open, and in front of them was the oddly shaped house where Robert and Jeanie lived.

'Mind you be on your best behaviour,' said her mother. 'Robert and Jeanie aren't used to children.'

'Why can't you stay,' Susie asked.

Her mother's face became sad. 'I'd love to stay with you, but I have to work, Susie – you know that.'

Susie didn't remember much about her father. She only knew him from the photo that stood on the mantelpiece in an ornate gilt frame. Every night before bedtime her mother would bring it down for Susie to 'kiss your daddy goodnight.' The story she'd been told had few details: he'd been a soldier, something had happened to him in the fighting during the war and he hadn't come home when the war ended.

After a cup of tea and a slice of homemade cake, her mother hugged her, saying, 'I must be off to catch the boat. I'll see you soon, Susie.'

It was so quiet on the island, especially at night when all that could be heard was the hoot of an owl somewhere in the trees and the faint whoosh of the water as it lapped around the shores of the distant bay.

She was used to falling asleep to the reassuring clang of the tramcars trundling up and down Argyle Street and on Saturdays to the shouts of revellers as they spilled out from the pub on the corner, laughing and singing loudly, but after the first night or two she became used to the silence, came to take pleasure in the lack of noise.

This house was much bigger than their room and kitchen in Glasgow and although Uncle Robert and Auntie Jeanie were very kind, they were strict and she wasn't allowed to go exploring on her own, venture up the dusty winding road that stretched as far as she could see.

'No, it's not allowed,' was the stock response whenever she asked.

At the time she didn't think to ask who might not 'allow' it and though not a timid child, Susie knew how important it was to her mother that she did as she was told. Besides, they were so kind, made a great fuss of her, keeping the tiny attic room at the top of the house, 'just for you, Susie, the way you like it.'

She started skipping again.

'Katie Bairdie had a coo,
It was yellow, black and blue
Open the gate and let it through,
Hurrah for Katie Bairdie.'

In a few weeks she would be back in Glasgow, snug with her mother in their own home, at school with her friends and the holiday on Bute would be over for another year, no more than a distant memory.

She would return the following summer as usual. Unless something happened, of course.

CHAPTER ONE

Susie Littlejohn stared at the letter, then turned the envelope over to study the postmark. The word *Rothesay* was clearly visible over the stamps.

She carried the letter out to the deck overlooking the shimmering blue water of the swimming pool of her rented apartment in Los Angeles and settled down on the lounger, trying to take in this sudden piece of news. Straightening the bandana holding her tumble of dark curls off her face, she peered over her sunglasses to read the correspondence from Inheritors Limited yet again.

"Dear Ms Littlejohn,

Property at Ettrick Bay, Isle of Bute.

Further to our recent correspondence and completion of our investigations we are pleased to confirm that you are indeed the sole heir to the above property.

All negotiations will be conducted through Messrs Laidlaw and Company, Montague Street, Rothesay."

She read no further. She'd studied this letter so often she knew it by heart and she laid it on the table in front of her, gazing into the distance. It had been a long time since she'd thought about that house high on the hill above Ettrick Bay and ages since she'd thought about her aunt and uncle, but reading the letter brought the memories flooding back.

When had she last been there? She closed her eyes and tried counting back the years, finally deciding she must have been no more than seven years old on her final visit. She recalled how she'd been taken there every summer to stay with her relatives. With her father dead, her mother had no option but to work and the long summer holidays were impossible to cover without help. They had been happy times, she recalled with a smile, though she had missed much about city life.

Dear Aunt Jeanie and Uncle Robert. She remembered them fondly. Her uncle had been a small, rotund, jovial man, while her aunt had been tall and thin – an odd pair they made, though as a child this thought hadn't occurred to her.

With no children of their own, they'd been delighted to welcome her, let her have her own room, her own place in their home. How she'd loved the tiny attic room at the top of the house, with its leaded window and the seat with the yellow cushion where she'd sit and gaze at a sky of stars, so clear and sharp without the loom from the city lights.

She frowned at the memory of the only disagreement she'd had with her uncle. As an adventurous child she'd been eager to go further than the limits of the garden round the house, but every time she asked, she'd been met with a firm, 'No.'

They'd been more than a little overprotective, forbidding her to explore as she wanted and, always mindful of her mother's warnings to 'do as you're told', Susie reluctantly obeyed.

And now it would appear they had died and left her that very house. A pang of guilt struck her. Why had she not kept in touch? In a sudden flashback she remembered that last summer. Her mother had been unusually quiet on the bus trip back to Rothesay and on the steamer, all the way across the Firth of Clyde and up to Glasgow, saying little in response to her daughter's chatter. She soon found out why. She'd returned home to find the picture of her father, the one that had had pride of place on top of the mantelpiece, had disappeared and her mother had introduced her to the tall man sitting in the big chair in the corner as 'your new daddy.'

At the time this had greatly puzzled her. How could you have a 'new daddy?' But her mother seemed happy, very happy. Susie remembered the day her mother had said, 'I've given up my job, Susie. I can be here for you all the time now.'

And Walter was exactly like a father to her. She couldn't recall her real father at all.

Gradually the contact with the relations on Bute had dwindled to a Christmas card and a present on her birthday. Then that too stopped. From this distance in time Susie guessed it was probably because the 'new daddy' didn't want to be reminded of the 'old daddy' and connections had been severed.

She sighed and folded up the letter. There was no way she could go rushing home to Scotland to claim her inheritance, at least not at the moment, yet a niggle of curiosity wouldn't go away.

Was the house as she remembered? It had seemed large to her as a child, but then that was one of the penalties of growing up; all the places of your childhood seemed to shrink in size. More importantly - why had it been left to her...and why now?

There had to be a way of settling this, of finding answers to these questions. She sat in the shade, hoping to be inspired, to come up with a plan.

At this time in the afternoon the breeze drifted up from the Pacific Ocean, taking the sting out of the dry desert heat and she sipped her cold drink, enjoying the satisfaction of being outside, one of the many pleasures of life in the kind Californian climate.

Who could help her? In a flash of inspiration she knew exactly who she could ask - her long-time friend, Alison Cameron. She reached for her phone. 'Alison, it's Susie.'

No sooner had she spoken than she realised it might have been better to email first, or at least check what time it was in Scotland. The note of panic in Alison's, 'Susie! Is everything all right?' reminded her that her best friend from their college days had a tendency always to imagine the worst in any situation.

'I'm absolutely fine, so don't be concerned.'

A sigh at the other end of the phone as Susie hurried on, 'I've had a letter, Alison and I'm looking for help. Do you remember I told you about how I used to go and stay on Bute when I was a child? About my aunt and uncle?'

'Mmm.' Alison's guarded response indicated she'd only the vaguest recollection of the conversation, thought Susie as she continued, 'I haven't had contact with them for years, but it appears they've died and left their little house to me.'

There was a long silence. Across the miles Susie could almost feel Alison trying to decide how best to reply, so she went on, scarcely pausing for breath, 'It's only a small house, though it seemed big to me as a child.'

No response. 'Looks like I've a holiday home on Bute,' she said to break the silence.

'I'm delighted for you,' replied Alison at last, 'and I'm sure it will be great for you when you come back home. You'll be looking forward to reviving happy memories. When are you thinking of returning?'

Susie bit her lip, hesitating before replying, 'That's the problem, Alison. I hoped you might be able to help me. Perhaps you could go down to Bute and look at the house? The negotiations are in the hands of one of the lawyers on the island...' she consulted the letter... 'a Mr Laidlaw whose office is in Montague Street in Rothesay.'

'This isn't the kind of thing you can pass on to someone else, Susie. You'd be better arranging to come over, as soon as you have a break from school.' Alison sounded cross.

'Please, please, Alison,' Susie implored, regretting again her decision to phone instead of emailing first. 'If you and Simon could go down and check it out for me? I'm sure it will all be straightforward. They were relatives of my mother, from what I remember, and they had no children, so there won't be any other claimants. There can't be many problems with a holiday home on Bute.

It's impossible to leave America at short notice. I've a full teaching timetable at the school here.'

This wasn't strictly true, thought Susie with a pang of guilt. The school would be accommodating if she presented this as some kind of crisis, but there was more than her job to think about. The relationship with Howard was going so well at the moment and she did have a number of other commitments it would be difficult to abandon, including the school musical she'd rashly volunteered to help stage.

There was another pause before Alison said grudgingly, 'I suppose Simon and I might enjoy a trip to Bute, even in February. It's a while since we visited the island. But you'll have to tell me more about this house of yours.'

'I don't remember much about it,' said Susie, 'but we – or rather I – did spend a lot of time there during the summer months when I was young. I must have been about six or seven the last time we visited, so the details are hazy. I do remember my attic bedroom and playing outside the house in the garden and occasional trips down to Ettrick Bay.'

'And that's it?'

'Sorry, that's all that comes to mind. I can't believe I'm the new owner.' Yet again the strangeness of this sudden inheritance struck her.

Alison was persistent. 'Can't you remember anything else about it?'

'Not really. I've no idea why we stopped going down there, though my mother's remarriage might have had something to do with it. I haven't been back to Bute since.'

Little shards of memory began to creep in: the photo of her father on the mantelpiece at home, the trip on the steamer, belching smoke as it made its way to the island, a vague recollection of the bus trip and the shop where they sold the best ice cream on the island. Where was that? Rothesay? Or Port Bannatyne?

Aware it was growing late in Scotland, Susie shook off these recollections and said before Alison could change her mind, 'I'm so grateful for your help. I'll email all the details and we can chat about it again. I'll have to organise permission for you to act on my behalf, but I'm sure that won't be too much of a problem.'

Susie put the phone down and began to examine the letter again in case she'd missed something.

How strange she should be the one to inherit, even if Robert and Jeanie had no children and she tried to recall what she knew about the rest of the family, which was very little.

If only she'd asked more questions when her mother was still alive. Growing up she'd no memory of hearing of other siblings. But then after her mother remarried it was likely contact with her family might have been limited, especially if they didn't live nearby. If indeed it was her mother's family. It was all such a muddle. Never mind, Alison would sort it out. She was good at that kind of thing.

Suddenly aware of the time, she jumped up and stuffed the letter into her bag. Howard would be arriving soon and she hadn't changed out of her school clothes. Not that there was much formality about how teachers and pupils dressed in the Thomas Paine High School in Los Angeles, a refreshing change from the strict uniform required of pupils at Strathelder High in her home town of Glasgow.

She grinned as she thought of the reaction had she turned up there in the bright yellow culottes and patterned top she'd decided on that morning. Even so, she'd welcome a shower and a change of outfit. Howard had promised her '…an evening to remember. We'll drive along the Pacific coast road down to Venice Beach and have dinner at the Oyster Bar and Grill in Market Street. It's world famous.'

She opened the patio doors of the kitchen enjoying the feel of the cool stone tiles on her bare feet, wondering what to wear. He'd given little hint other than telling her about the restaurant, but they'd probably stroll round the canals before dinner and afterwards have a walk along the Ocean

Front Boardwalk to see the various acts performing there, the acrobats and the singers, or sit idly watching the strangely attired residents, of which there were many. She rummaged in her closet. Comfortable shoes were a must.

Yes. There were lots of things she liked about living here. Now if only everything would work out with Howard, she could easily see herself staying here much longer than the current year's exchange she'd signed up for. Surely that would be possible to arrange without too much difficulty.

The thought appealed to her greatly and she began to sing as she headed for the shower. She was so looking forward to the evening. Whatever her decision about the house on Bute, it could wait for the moment.

CHAPTER TWO

'Sorry about that, Alison. I should have realised you'd need more information.'

'Of course I do, Susie. This is all terribly vague and when I'd time to think about it I came to the conclusion we couldn't possibly turn up at the lawyer's and claim we were your friends with consent to take possession of this house on Bute. We need to know a lot more about it and it was made pretty clear that there's no way a cursory email will be enough.'

Susie sighed. As usual, Alison was right. 'I'll tell you what I know. I have sent a letter giving you permission to act on my behalf – it's all official and done through a lawyer in Glasgow. I don't want to bore you with the details.'

'I'm sitting in the lounge with a glass of wine, so take as long as you like,' said Alison.

'Well, here goes, but there are a lot of fine points I'm pretty sketchy on myself. Do you remember me talking about the Ainslees? I've found out through Inheritors Limited that my mother was a relative, a distant one from what I can gather, though I knew them as my aunt and my uncle. I guess the way things were after my father died, my mother thought herself lucky to have someone to help. She was an only child, so there was no one in her immediate family to take me on during the holidays.'

'I've a dim memory of you saying something about it,' said Alison. 'I seem to recall you telling me about the relatives you visited in the summer.' It was clear Alison was being tactful and remembered little of the conversation.

'And so...?'

Recognising a note of impatience in Alison's voice, Susie hurried on, 'Well, I was surprised as anyone to get the call from Inheritors Limited: they track down missing heirs. I thought it was a joke at first, or one of those telephone scams, but no, it was true. Apparently Robert and his wife had no children. I heard some story about his first wife and the baby dying in childbirth and I guess he never re-married. Aunt Jeanie wasn't his wife at all, I have to suppose. Not a problem now, but a scandal then.'

'And there were no other relatives?'

'Apparently not, though I've no idea how extensive the research was. All I had to do was meet with the representative, sign up with Inheritors Limited and that was it.'

'But don't you want to see the house?'

'Of course I do, but it's not that simple, Alison.' Susie fiddled with one of her long dangling earrings as she spoke, well aware the version of events she was giving Alison was only partly fact laced with a fair amount of surmise.

Truth was she didn't know much about these relatives. She'd only ever known them as Uncle Robert and Aunt Jeanie and once she stopped going to Bute they had become no more than a distant memory, never again mentioned as far as she could recall.

Her mother was long dead, as was her stepfather. She did have some of their personal papers, but those were stowed in boxes in the cupboard back in her flat in Glasgow. Besides, it was hard to imagine there might be anything relevant.

Ah, well, with a bit of luck Alison would sort it all out. Meantime Susie had other matters on her mind, mostly to do with Howard.

CHAPTER THREE

Occupied as she was with the problem of her relationship with Howard, Susie didn't give the inheritance of a holiday home at Ettrick Bay much thought after her phone call to Alison. While it was rather nice to know there was a bolt-hole on the Isle of Bute, she might want to sell it rather than keep it, especially if her plans with Howard worked out. And how expensive would it be to maintain a house she seldom used?

There are enough complications in my life, Susie told herself as she heard her cell phone ping. There, as though on cue, was a text from Howard. She frowned as she read it.

'Sorry, can't make it tonight. H x'

No reason, no excuse. Her heart gave a little lurch. Was it possible he was growing tired of her? Surely not. Whenever they met he seemed so loving, so caring, determined she would enjoy whatever new ploy he'd come up with for her amusement.

I must ignore these doubts, she said aloud, as if to reassure herself. It's all my imagination. He has a busy job as a realtor and from what he'd said on more than one occasion, clients could be very demanding, especially in this part of the world. Several times he'd had to call off at short notice because someone had demanded an immediate appointment to view a property. She sighed. In the short time she'd been working in the country she'd learned Americans worked very hard.

No sooner had she shut down her phone, trying to ignore the empty feeling in the pit of her stomach, than the sound of Under the Boardwalk heralded a call. She felt her spirits soar. Ah, she had misjudged him. That would surely be Howard with an explanation for calling off their planned excursion to Topanga Canyon. She looked at the screen and for a moment didn't recognise the number, but only for a moment.

'Hello, Susie,' said Alison.

'Oh, it's you?'

'Were you expecting another caller?'

Susie hesitated, because Alison sounded troubled, then she said, 'Hi, Alison. Sorry – I didn't expect to hear from you so soon. How did it go?'

Was that a note of caution she detected in Alison's next words? 'Well, Susie, there are no immediate problems.' There was a brief pause before she went on,' It's just that, well, the place is a bit bigger than I expected. But perhaps it's because I didn't fully understand what you were telling me about the house.'

'What do you mean, Alison? I know it appeared big to me as a child, but it's no more than a cottage.'

There was a sharp intake of breath at the other end of the phone. 'Yes, there is a house, a lodge house, that's true. But it's more...rather it's what's attached to the lodge house.'

Susie felt a wave of impatience. Kind as Alison was to take on the task of sorting out her inheritance, in spite of his text Howard might phone at any minute and she didn't want to miss the call. All she had to know was that everything had gone smoothly on Bute, with no hiccups.

Suddenly an image of the house in a dilapidated state flashed into her mind. That was the difficulty, of course. Alison and Simon had gone to look at the place and far from a lovely seaside retreat, they'd found a house that was in terrible condition, needing lots of money to restore it.

'Oh, for goodness sake, Alison, stop beating about the bush and tell me what's happening. No matter how bad it is, there's nothing I can do about it at the moment.'

As Alison described in great detail what Susie had become heir to, she felt her heart beginning to beat faster and faster.

'The house you remember is only the lodge house, Susie. There's more to it than that...much more. The main building is a large Victorian manor, much the worse for wear, but it's honestly huge.'

'What! You're joking. Surely there must be some mistake.'

'No, Susie, there's no mistake. It's all yours. I suspect when you visited as a child for some reason you lived in the lodge house: the main house is well screened by trees, so you may not have been aware there was another building further up the driveway.'

A picture of a long dusty road leading away from the lodge came to mind, a road she'd been forbidden to explore. Why on earth were her relations living in such a small house if they owned a Victorian mansion?

She tried to think of a way to reply to this bewildering news as Alison continued, 'I thought that, in the circumstances, you might want to come over and see for yourself.'

'You know I can't,' wailed Susie. 'I'm at a critical stage in sorting out the continuation of this job...'

Aware she might give too much away, Susie let her voice tail off. But she and Alison had been friends for too long for such pretence.

'And,' said Alison, 'what is happening that you're not telling me about?'

No point in lying, thought Susie. Alison had guessed correctly that the exchange was only one of the reasons she was putting off coming back to Scotland.

She said, 'Well, while it's true about the job – I'm committed to helping with the school musical - there is this man that I've been seeing. Nothing serious you understand, but I don't really want to come away at the moment. Our relationship has reached a certain stage, if you know what I mean.'

Judging by the firm tone she adopted, Alison was clearly impatient with this reply. 'Susie, I don't think you understand. This is a mansion you've been left...and that's in addition to the lodge house. It's a huge property and there are decisions to be made. I can help, but I've so much to do at the moment and...'

Susie cut in before Alison could begin a long litany of her many activities. 'Please, please, Alison, I do need your assistance. This is a great opportunity for me here and I don't want to mess it up. The house will still be there when I come back. It's stood empty for some time and a while longer won't cause any difficulty.'

'Oh, so you are planning to return?'

'Don't worry, Alison. You know I'll have to come back at some point, especially if I don't get an extension of my permit. Please, please help me. I'm sure you can manage things until June and I'll have to come back then anyway.'

To Susie's relief Alison relented, saying, 'Fine, Susie, I'll speak to Simon about it, but no more than that. I'll phone you at the weekend to let you know our decision.'

Profuse in her thanks, Susie chatted for a few more minutes asking questions about Alison's family before saying, 'Thanks so much. This means a lot to me.'

As Alison signed off she said, 'And don't forget to check your email regularly. If there's anything else you need to know I'll be in touch immediately.'

Susie felt a wave of relief as she snapped her phone shut. Of course Alison thought it strange she didn't want to rush home immediately to see this great inheritance, but Susie had a horrible feeling it would amount to no more than a lot of trouble if the place was as rundown as Alison suggested. Besides it all seemed so remote somehow, in time as well as place. She'd settled in well in America, felt very much at home.

But now she had learned the extent of her inheritance, there were more questions than answers. The more she thought about it, the less she seemed to know. She bit her thumb then hastily stopped, aware of how much she'd paid for a French manicure the day before.

The same question kept going round and round in her head. Why had her aunt and uncle lived in the lodge house if they'd owned a huge mansion? Had it been abandoned because they couldn't afford the upkeep?

She shuddered. If it was as neglected as she suspected she might well be liable for any costs involved in knocking it down.

She really didn't need this complication in her life at the moment. In spite of her decision to leave Alison to sort it out, she would have to do some investigating to find out why this huge Victorian pile had been left to her.

If Robert and Jeanie did own the mansion Alison described, how had they acquired it? They weren't rich by any means, else why were they living in the little house at the bottom of the drive. It was all very strange.

CHAPTER FOUR

'Gee, what a great thing,' said Ethel.

Susie smiled at her friend. Since taking up her year's exchange post at the Thomas Paine High School she'd made a number of friends, but Ethel was the closest.

'I know.' Susie shrugged. 'I only wish I'd a better idea about why I was the one to inherit.'

'Chill! Stop worrying about it. If I'd been left a place like you describe I'd be well delighted.'

In spite of Ethel's words of comfort, Susie had this underlying feeling of doubt. There must surely be some mistake. The lodge house she could understand, but a Victorian mansion? She gazed at her computer screen, scanning every last detail of the picture Alison had emailed over. It had a curious air of unreality. The house looked as if it was solidly built of stone and from the front view the number of windows gave some indication of how large it was. She peered closely at the screen, enlarging the picture as best she could without making it look too fuzzy. Mmm. It was certainly in need of some loving attention, judging by the long grass and the evidence of ivy smothering the walls.

She sat back. This wasn't getting her any further forward. She had to make a list of questions and then her first port of call should be Inheritors Limited. After all, they had tracked her down, no doubt for a large fee, so they should have the information she needed.

Trouble was, there were so many questions to ask, but if she took it slowly, sent a preliminary request, that would be a start.

She took some time to compose the email, redoing it three times before she was satisfied. There was so much she wanted to know, but an email wasn't the place.

In the end she decided it would be better to be brief and wrote

'Reference 5641 Ettrick House, Isle of Bute.

As the recent inheritor of Ettrick House on the Isle of Bute, I should be grateful for more information about the previous owners of the property who I believe were relatives of my mother. I am currently working in America and would be pleased to arrange a suitable time to call you.'

It wasn't ideal, but should surely prompt them into action. She pressed SEND before she could have second thoughts.

The phone rang and so engrossed was she, it was a moment or two before she realised. She pressed the answer button in time to hear Ethel say, 'Susie, how do you fancy meeting in Smokey Joe's bar in the Westfield shopping Mall? You know, that place we went to a couple of weeks ago.'

Susie glanced at her watch. She didn't want to refuse Ethel, but she was supposed to be meeting

Howard in an hour and if she accepted Ethel's offer, she'd be running late.

'Sorry, Ethel, could we make it another time? I have to meet Howard soon.'

There was a long pause. 'Honey, that's what I want to talk to you about.'

Susie felt a chill run through her. 'What's happened? Has he had an accident?'

'No, nothing like that,' Ethel hurried to reassure her. 'Look, Susie, I wouldn't be so insistent if it weren't important.'

Even in the short time she'd known her, Susie had come to trust Ethel completely, so she must have a good reason for wanting this urgent meeting.

Ethel had guided her through so many problems, so many difficulties, kept her from making social gaffes on many occasions since she'd taken up the post in America, but Susie couldn't think why Ethel might have something to tell her about Howard. As far as she knew, they were barely acquainted.

'Okay. I could have a quick drink with you.'

If she showered and changed now, she could go straight to meet Howard from the Mall. Besides, he was used to her being a little late on most occasions, 'An English quirk, no doubt,' he'd say. She didn't bother to correct his use of 'English.'

No time to dally over what she should wear – a comfortable pair of slacks and a new green top that set off the colour of her eyes, completed by a jacket she carried 'just in case' though in case of what she wasn't sure. The weather here was so predictable, but old habits and concern about the vagaries of the Scottish weather died hard.

Ethel was sitting in a corner booth at the far end of Smokey Joe's. The place was quiet at this time of the evening and the smart young waiter brought their mint juleps in record time.

'Cheers,' said Susie, made even more curious by the way Ethel didn't return the toast, but sipped at her drink as though putting off the moment she had to talk.

Susie leaned over and said, 'Ethel, I know you invited me here for a reason. Do you want to tell me what's going on? I'm bursting with curiosity.'

Ethel shifted in her seat before she raised her eyes. 'I don't know how to tell you this. It's Howard, honey.'

'Yes, yes,' said Susie impatiently. 'What about Howard.'

'Do you know he's married...very married,' said Ethel. Her words came out in a rush.

Susie put her drink down on the table in front of her, her hand shaking as she did so. Without thinking she lifted one of the paper napkins from the box in front of her and began to mop up the little drops she'd spilled.

'What do you mean?' She was surprised how calm she sounded: inwardly she felt her heart gripped as though by a vice.

'I'm so sorry, Susie. I couldn't bear you not to know the truth. Every time you mention him, say how happy you are, I feel guilty.'

'Perhaps you've made a mistake?' As she spoke, Susie could tell from the way Ethel looked at her that she was clutching at straws.

Ethel shook her head and leaned over. 'No mistake, honey. And it's not the first time.'

'But how do you know? You're not a friend of his.' Susie couldn't help her sharp tone of voice as she tried to digest this news.

'Because someone I know well got entangled with him a couple of years ago and it came to grief. He's a,' she made quote marks in the air with her fingers, 'serial lover'. I had to tell you.'

'So who would that be?' Susie downed the rest of her drink.

Ethel refused to say, only adding, 'His poor wife either doesn't realise what's going on, or ignores it.'

Susie gazed into the distance, trying to decide if this could be true. What's more, she was beginning to suspect the 'friend' Ethel was talking about might be Ethel herself.

All around her, people were laughing, enjoying the atmosphere of Smokey Joe's, oblivious to her inner turmoil. It was a moment or two before she could bring herself to reply. 'So what do I do now?'

Ethel appeared embarrassed by this question. 'It's up to you. But I know what I'd do. Believe me, there's not a chance he'll leave his wife - can't afford the alimony. What's more this isn't his first wife.'

'Not his first wife? How many wives has he had?'

Susie stood up, trying to control her trembling. Suddenly she felt composed and distant as though this was happening to someone else, but all she could say was, 'Thanks, Ethel, for letting me know before I made even more of a fool of myself.'

Ethel grabbed her hand. 'I'm so sorry, Susie. I don't want you to end up with a broken heart.'

'I don't think it's that serious.' But she knew it was. Howard was such fun, so keen to help her get to know this part of America and beyond. In spite of herself, she'd had this hope that it might be more than a short-term romance. That he had been less than honest with her was hard to understand.

She said goodbye to Ethel, judging the coolness between them would be remedied next time they met. The problem now was, should she believe what Ethel had told her and if so what should she do about Howard?

CHAPTER FIVE

Firstly, thought Susie, I have to avoid panicking. She took a deep breath. Howard must have a very good reason for cancelling yet again. What I must do, she told herself sternly, is go through the sequence of events since meeting him, look for any clues that Ethel was telling the truth.

She clung on to the hope that Ethel was wrong. She must have mixed him up with someone else, someone with the same name.

She ticked off everything she knew on her fingers, speaking aloud as she did so.

'Firstly, he was the one who approached me.' She stopped to consider what had happened that evening when she'd been invited to a barbeque at the house of one of the other teachers. Howard had homed in on her immediately and hadn't left her alone all evening. They'd laughed later at how they'd talked at cross purposes. She thought he was one of the teachers, he thought he was there in a professional capacity, to interest her in renting one of the company properties. There had been no sign, no indication, of a wife.

'Secondly, he persisted even when I said I wasn't too sure.'

What she had actually said was, 'I'm only here for a year's exchange and I don't want to become involved in a relationship that can only come to grief.'

He'd laughed at her concerns. 'Sweetheart, we all live for the moment. Let's see how it goes.'

And she'd had to admit it would be foolish to miss out on an opportunity with someone with whom she'd so much in common because of concerns about the future.

She frowned as she said, 'Thirdly, he couldn't have been more attentive.'

If it hadn't been for Howard, she wouldn't have seen anything like the number of sights of California that she had. Oh, the friends she made at school were very kind, but they all led busy lives, whereas Howard seemed free to take her around. And take her around he had – down to Santa Monica pier, through the Getty Centre, out to Universal studios and even to a Baseball game at the Dodger Stadium.

But now something was wrong. She could feel it, sense it. Trouble was she wasn't sure what. And to add to her woes she'd received a reply from Inheritors Limited in response to her query about Ettrick House.

It was in the mailbox when she'd arrived back from school and now it lay on the table in front of her, daring her to open it.

Putting all thoughts of Howard to one side, she crossed to the tiny kitchen that formed part of the living area of her apartment. It was such an ideal place to live, with the patio doors opening out on to a deck overlooking the communal grounds and the swimming pool.

She perked some coffee, an addiction Howard had introduced her to, instead of the tea she'd once preferred. Whatever happened with their relationship, she'd never be quite the same person again.

With a large black coffee in front of her, she sat down at the breakfast bar and opened the letter.

'Dear Miss Littlejohn,

Reference 5641 Ettrick House, Isle of Bute.

In response to your query regarding the reasons for your inheriting the above property, I am sorry to advise you we can be of little further assistance.

Our remit is to track down heirs where a property is left with no will attached and therefore no indication of the line of inheritance.

Our records show that the property was originally owned by Robert Ainslee and following on his death passed to Robert Fraser as custodian. As there were no children, the property falls to you as the next in line.

I suggest you contact the Scottish Records Office for further details.'

That was no help, thought Susie. They seemed to be very cavalier about the process. No doubt now they'd earned their commission they weren't the least bit interested in spending time answering her questions.

She put the letter aside and sipped her coffee. There must be a way to deal with this. The problem was she was so far away and though Alison had been ready to lend a hand, she detected in the last email a certain frisson about helping further.

She couldn't blame her friend. Alison had been busy on her behalf, but her last email had mentioned a further tricky situation that was down to Susie to sort out. For some reason a team of archaeologists had been given permission to dig in the grounds of Ettrick House. Another complication.

She picked up the letter and read it again, scanning it for some clue that might help her make progress. But no, there was nothing.

Wait a minute. How could she have missed that? Who on earth was Robert Fraser? She'd inherited the house from her uncle, Robert Ainslee, who was a relative of her mother and she was certain she'd never heard the name Fraser mentioned. What was her uncle's relationship to Robert Fraser? Could Inheritors Limited have made a mistake and got the name wrong? That seemed most unlikely.

There were lots of questions, but no answers. But it couldn't be clearer – here was a mystery she'd have to investigate ...and soon.

CHAPTER SIX

In the end the decision was made for her. Susie tossed and turned all night after Ethel's revelation, rising before dawn to go out on to the deck with a cup of coffee, watching the sky lighten to the promise of another hot day.

As it was Saturday there was no school to worry about. She'd planned to go to the beach with a couple of the teachers from Thomas Paine High, take a picnic and make the most of the warm weather.

I can't leave it like this, thought Susie. There's no way I can pretend everything is the same. I have to try to find out the truth, discover if Ethel is right and he is a married man. She'd seen too many friends go that route, most to be sadly disappointed, often after many years of waiting in the hope of graduating from being the mistress to being the wife.

Of course, she didn't have such expectations about Howard...or did she? She sipped her coffee, idly watching a little hummingbird flit to and fro in the pink froth of the Californian fuchsia in the patch of garden at the far end of the pool, all the while trying to decide her next move.

The house phone rang and she put her cup on the table, almost dropping it in her haste to go indoors.

'Hiya, Sweetheart.' In spite of her misgivings her heart gave a little skip at the sound of Howard's voice. 'Thought I'd give you a call. What do you say to a trip out to the mountains this weekend? I know it's kinda short notice...'

'Sorry,' said Susie, cutting in. 'I've made plans for today.'

There was a noticeable chill in his voice as Howard said, 'Oh, so you're not around then?'

Drat, thought Susie, I shouldn't have been so hasty to make arrangements. Then she took a deep breath. Surely he didn't expect her to be the kind of woman who'd sit around on the off chance he'd call?

'I thought you worked Saturdays?'

He chuckled. 'Usually I do, but I managed to engineer this one off.'

Susie thought quickly. 'I'm free tomorrow?'

'Mmm, sorry, Sweetheart. Got to go in to catch up on some paperwork.'

Susie had a sudden feeling of deflation. What's more, Ethel's words rang in her ears. Did he really have to go into the office on a Sunday?

She took a deep breath. 'Can't you do the paperwork today and we could go off somewhere tomorrow?'

His voice was as smooth as silk as he replied without a moment's hesitation, 'Uh, uh. It doesn't work like that, Susie.'

But she was determined to sort this out. 'Let's arrange another time then. Sometime during next week? Even for a quick drink?'

After some discussion they settled on the following Tuesday at the Bar Pinto in downtown L.A. but Howard signed off leaving Susie less than happy.

She hadn't noticed it before, or if she had she'd chosen to ignore it, but Howard was unwilling to commit himself too far in advance. Oh, he always made the excuse that he was a 'slave to the clients' but this time she didn't believe him.

With a heavy heart, sensing the end of the affair, Susie went through to the bedroom to get ready for the trip to the beach. Perhaps a day out with friends would take her mind off her troubles. She was glad Ethel wouldn't be there.

CHAPTER SEVEN

It took Susie a few minutes to spot Howard in the far corner of the Pinto Nuevo in downtown Los Angeles as she came in from the brightness of the afternoon. The dim lighting made this bar a favourite spot for Angelinos keen to escape the heat and the glare of a Californian day.

He was hunched over a beer, chilled in the way he liked, judging by the rivulets of cold on the glass.

He stood up to greet her, kissing her on the cheek. 'Hi, Sweetheart, good to see you,' he smiled, crinkling up his eyes in the way that set her heart racing.

The waitress appeared silently beside them and Susie ordered, 'Diet Coke, please, no ice.'

Howard raised an eyebrow. 'You on the wagon?' adding to the waitress, 'Another beer for me, ice-cold.'

Susie shook her head. 'I fancy a soft drink,' she said, but the truth was she wanted to keep a clear head and with Howard one drink could easily lead to another.

The drinks arrived quickly and she took a few moments to sip hers while Howard watched her. The trouble with me, thought Susie, is that I find it difficult to disguise my feelings.

They sat in silence for a few moments until she could stand the suspense no longer. Taking a deep breath she blurted out, 'There's something I want to talk to you about, Howard.'

A look of alarm crossed his face and then he burst out laughing. 'Oh, Susie, don't frighten me. It worries me when you look so serious.'

He leaned across the table and took her hand, but she swiftly pulled it away, clasping both hands round her glass.

'No, Howard, there is something I'd like to discuss with you and I'd appreciate an honest answer.'

Howard shifted in his seat, not meeting her eye as he replied, 'Sure, Sweetheart, I'll do my best. But I can't imagine what it could possibly be to make you seem so solemn.'

He sipped his beer, and began watching her warily over the rim of his glass.

Now that the moment had come, Susie couldn't think where to begin without sounding stupid. She should have given this more consideration. 'It's about our relationship, Howard,' she began, realising how clichéd that sounded, but she got no further as he interrupted her with a laugh, 'I thought we were getting along just fine.'

Oh, what did it matter? Best to come straight out with it. 'Howard, are you married?'

For a moment she thought he was going to deny it, which would have been a relief.

Instead he made a face. 'I guess you had to know sometime. Yes, I am married, Susie.' This time there was no 'Sweetheart'.

Susie sat still, unable to speak, waiting for the usual excuses. 'My wife and I don't get on,' or 'We've been living apart,' or even the classic, 'My wife doesn't understand me,' but he said none of these, letting the silence stretch between them.

He sipped his beer and all she could manage was, 'Where does that leave us?'

Tempted as she was to say more, to question him intently, Susie bit back the words, waiting for him to explain.

He shrugged at her question, still making no response.

Incensed by his attitude, Susie quelled her inclination to lean over the table, wrest the beer from his hands and punch him.

'That's it then?'

He opened his hands in a gesture as if to say, 'So what?' but then he spoke, 'I didn't ever tell you I wasn't married, Susie.'

'How ridiculous,' she shouted, all attempts at a reasonable discussion abandoned, ignoring the interest she was generating in the other customers, several of whom turned round to stare at this spate. 'You don't go out with someone and the first question you ask is, 'Are you married?' do you?'

'I guess not.' Howard's calm demeanor was infuriating and she stood up. This was impossible. All she could do now was exit with dignity.

'In that case, it's over, Howard. Kindly don't get in touch again.'

To her intense annoyance, he made no attempt to detain her, kept staring at the table to avoid her gaze. 'If that's the way you want it, Sweetheart.'

Susie almost ran out of the bar, grateful they'd chosen this place where no one knew her. She stumbled out into the glare of the afternoon. Damn Howard. What did she care, except that he'd deceived her? It was fine to say he'd never actually lied, but did he believe she'd have become involved with him if she'd known? Of course not.

She wiped away her tears and hailed a passing cab, scarcely managing to give her address without breaking down again.

Well, that settled it. As the streets passed in a blur she made up her mind. Half-term was coming up soon. She had intended to spend it with Howard, but now she'd go to the Travel Agent first thing in the morning and book a flight to Glasgow.

She'd head for Bute to have a look at this Victorian mansion she'd inherited. She wouldn't tell Alison she was coming. She'd only fuss. Let it be a surprise.

CHAPTER EIGHT

As she made the journey by train from Central Station in Glasgow to Wemyss Bay, glimmers of memory returned and the journey on the ferry across to Rothesay felt like stepping back in time. Much had changed over the years, but the sweep of the bay, the houses appearing to sit perilously on the hill above, these sights recalled the journeys she had made so long ago with her mother.

Taking the bus from Guildford Square was a memory too far and she managed to get the last taxi in the stand to take her to Ettrick House.

'Visiting, are you?' said the taxi driver.

'Mmm, you could say that,' she replied and opened her phone as though to check for messages. While she didn't want to appear rude, she couldn't face engaging in speculation about the place she'd inherited and it was with some relief she recognised the large gates at the entrance to the property, though she couldn't help but gasp as they made their way up the drive and Ettrick House came into view.

Alison hadn't been exaggerating: this impressive three storey building commanded a central position amid extensive grounds, but as they drew closer, Susie could see the iron balconies were perilously rusted, the front gardens overgrown, flower beds choked with weeds. She didn't dare gaze at the roof, suspecting it might need more than minor repairs.

'Some place, eh? Though I wouldn't fancy the heating bills,' said the taxi driver to which she could only whisper, 'Sure is,' in reply.

She got out of the taxi and paid the driver, adding a generous tip to make up for her silence on the journey.

She scarcely noticed the chipped stone lions guarding the doorway as she climbed the steps. Yes, Alison had told her about the house, had sent over photos, but somehow the reality far exceeded anything she could have imagined.

She knocked on the door, realising too late that her great plan of surprising Alison might backfire. What if they weren't here, weren't on the island? There was no sign of a car, but it might be parked at the back of the property. She gazed around as she waited and over in the distance she could see a flurry of activity that could only be the archaeologists. That was a problem for later.

She knocked again, more insistently this time and suddenly the door was pulled open. Alison stood there motionless. If Susie had intended to surprise her friend, it was clear she had succeeded.

'Hi, Alison, I bet you're astonished to see me,' she laughed.

'Good heavens, Susie. We didn't expect you.' Alison stood aside to let Susie in.

'I didn't anticipate being here,' said Susie as Alison led her through to what appeared to be the room she and Simon were using as a living area.

'We thought you were the archaeologists,' said Simon by way of explaining the tea tray with several mugs he was carrying. He didn't give the impression of being as stunned as Alison was, but Susie knew him as a man who wasn't easily rattled.

'Let me look at you,' said Alison, holding Susie at arm's length. She frowned. 'Are you okay? Have you been out in the sun too long?'

Susie laughed loudly. 'It's not real, Alison: it's all out of a bottle. Or rather a very expensive tanning salon near Venice Beach.'

'Good grief,' Alison said. 'Why would you want to do that with the weather they have in California?'

Susie wagged her finger. 'It's much too dangerous to sit out in the sun for any length of time. Yet you must have a tan.'

'Let Susie at least have a cup of tea before you interrogate her,' said Simon, lifting one of the mugs.

'You've been too long in L.A.' Alison appeared reluctant to let drop the subject of Susie's strange colour.

'Never mind that, Alison: I want you to tell me what's been happening here.'

Alison glanced over at Simon before replying. 'There have been some developments. The archaeologists have found a skeleton.'

'A skeleton! Oh, Alison, I'm so sorry. When I asked you to come over to check out the house, I'd no idea it would involve you in all this.'

'It's not been a problem, Susie. It's only that...' Alison gestured wildly, 'all this seems to have assumed a momentum of its own.'

'But whose is the skeleton?' Susie insisted.

Alison shook her head. 'According to the archaeologists the skeleton has been in the ground for hundreds of years. It happens to be well preserved, but don't worry - it's not recent. You can speak to them later. They are very friendly and they haven't caused us any bother.'

Clearly the skeleton wasn't Alison's only concern. 'So what made you come back? I thought you didn't intend to return till the end of June?'

Susie let out a long sigh. 'Yes, I know. I thought so too. But it didn't work out as planned.'

Alison smiled. 'It, or him, Susie?'

'Both. It all seemed to be going so well: the job, the lifestyle, the romance.'

'And then?'

'I discovered he was married. He was still living with his wife and terrified of being found out. And too frightened of the alimony payments to divorce. Especially as he was paying alimony to his first wife. He was worried about his standing in the community.'

Alison raised her eyebrows, but didn't speak and Susie went on, 'Apart from the money issues he was concerned his wife might spill the beans about him if they split up. From what my friend, Ethel, hinted at, there were some shady dealings in his property business.'

At that moment Simon reappeared to announce, 'They've taken the skeleton away,' adding in response to Susie's question, 'The police won't be interested. Anything over seventy-five years isn't investigated.'

Susie felt comforted as Simon explained the processes. 'Thank goodness. I don't like the idea of dead bodies on my land,' but her joke fell flat.

Alison suggested they go out for dinner, to the restaurant at Kilchattan Bay.

'Deborah has joined us for a while,' she said, 'so I expect she'll want to come to dinner.'

'It will be good to catch up with her,' Susie replied, not wishing to ask too many questions as to why Alison's younger daughter, an Art college student, should want to spend time on Bute. Guiltily she realised she hadn't asked after Alison's other children – her daughter Maura who lived in London and her son Alastair who was a lecturer at a university in Canada.

She tried to recall the details, but was saved by Alison saying, 'Let's go now. The Kingarth can be very busy and we haven't booked.'

Over dinner, Susie was happy to regale them with stories of her time in Los Angeles, though Alison was unusually quiet, and Deborah was the one who contributed most to the conversation.

But Susie wasn't as light-hearted as she appeared. In spite of Simon's reassurances, in spite of seeming happy about the solution to the problem of the skeleton, Susie was worried. She was no further forward in understanding why she had inherited Ettrick House. Whatever the reason, she now regretted asking Alison to become involved. It had only complicated matters.

She felt guilty about her decision. Alison had been more than kind in taking on the work of sorting out Ettrick House, but this was something she had to do on her own, a family puzzle she had to solve without help from her friend.

And perhaps, if she was being honest with herself, she wasn't as over Howard as she liked to pretend.

CHAPTER NINE

Susie felt there had to be some way of finding the information she needed and, in spite of initial setbacks, the opportunity came sooner than expected. Alison had decided a trip into Rothesay was needed. 'We seem to be using a lot of coffee,' she said. 'Simon is keeping the archaeologists going.'

Susie offered to go with her, trying to conceal her feelings of relief when Alison suggested she'd be better staying at the house 'in case of developments.'

Susie was convinced that a clue to this strange inheritance must lie within the house itself, and when Deborah announced she was going for a walk, Susie seized her chance.

'Will you be long?' she asked.

'Mmm...might look in at the excavation and see what progress they're making.'

As soon as she was on her own, Susie set to. Problem was, where should she look first? The house was so large, so sprawling. And then again, there was almost no furniture so it was unlikely that there would be anything of interest unless it was cleverly hidden.

Of course. The lodge house. She hadn't been down there since arriving. Compared with the size of Ettrick House, the lodge wasn't a problem. But this was where her aunt and uncle had lived and as far as she knew, it hadn't been cleared as Ettrick House had.

She grabbed her jacket from the hall and hurried out, checking she'd the key safely in her pocket before closing the front door behind her. She tiptoed down the stone steps. Yes, she'd been right. Over in the far corner of the site Deborah had stopped and was deep in conversation with the archaeologists.

With no idea when Alison would return, Susie was aware her time might be limited. At this stage best to keep everything to herself, not involve anyone else, at least not before she'd made some progress. Alison had been so ready to lend a hand, but Susie felt guilty about asking her friend for more help.

As she approached the lodge, memories came flooding back and she could almost see herself as a young child, playing in the garden at the front. Why hadn't she noticed something the size of Ettrick House? But when she reached the main door with its elaborately carved lintel and a date of 1850 and turned back to look, she realised the house was invisible from the lodge, screened by trees and disguised by the sweep and bend of the road leading up to it.

She could feel her heart begin to beat faster. 'Get a grip, Susie,' she said aloud to dispel any ghosts as she turned the key in the rusty lock, succeeding in opening the door on the third attempt. It was clear it had been shut tight for a long time.

Dust hung everywhere and as she stepped through the narrow hallway, setting motes dancing and whirling in the sunlight streaming in, she began to sneeze. The house was so much smaller than she remembered. To her child self it had appeared huge, but in reality it consisted of no more than a front room, a tiny dining room with a kitchen off. Had it not been for the dust and general air of decay, the place looked as if someone had walked out no more than a few moments before.

In the kitchen, the ancient cooker sported a couple of empty saucepans and the battered wooden dresser held an array of mismatched china. Good heavens, there was the bowl she'd used as a child, the one with Goldilocks and the Three Bears on it. She lifted it down, running her fingers over the picture, recalling the many times she'd been told to 'eat up all your porridge, so you'll see the bears at the bottom.'

This would never do. She'd only a short time before Alison returned and she hadn't begun to look for clues about her inheritance.

Where would her uncle keep important papers? She went back into the hallway to climb the short flight of wooden stairs up to the bedrooms.

The main bedroom with the large antique brass bed, still with its covers on, was exactly as she remembered, and then up a flight of shallow stairs was the small attic room that had been hers.

She sat down on the single bed, sneezing again as the dust rose. The wallpaper, patterned with animals was still the same, though much discoloured over time and the yellow cushion on the window seat, frayed round the edges, had faded to a bleached white.

As she sat there, a million questions came to mind. Why had this place not been cleared? Had it been forgotten about? Or perhaps her aunt and uncle had found the house too big and had sold off the furniture? But why do that and not sell the house?

If only she had a plan, she thought, not for the first time. No matter. What she had to do was write down everything she remembered and then a list of questions. Surely that lawyer – what was his name? Laidlaw, that was it. Surely he must have some information. Probably he felt he couldn't tell Alison everything, in spite of her credentials. A trip into Rothesay on her own was called for.

She looked at her watch to see that, while she had been lost in her memories, almost an hour had passed. There was no way she could continue her search now. Susie realised if she was to make any progress in finding out the truth, she had to be methodical. At least that was her intention.

She made her way downstairs, looked round once more, and with a sigh, she closed the front door carefully behind her.

CHAPTER TEN

Her first idea, to consult Mr. Laidlaw, had to be put on hold. Susie had guessed Alison might want to go off the island soon and then there would be lots of opportunity to find out more about Ettrick House.

So when Alison said she'd bumped into Harry Sneddon in the Ettrick Bay Tearoom, and that she'd arranged to visit him and his wife, Greta, Susie couldn't help but burst out, 'Alison, I don't see why you want us to spend the afternoon in the company of someone who's the gloomiest person on earth. Surely you remember how depressing even a few minutes with Harry could be when he taught with us at Strathelder High?'

But Alison was not prepared to back down and Susie, mindful of how willingly she had accepted

Alison's help, could only agree she would go, with words of warning, 'Only if the visit is short.'

As it turned out, to Susie's great surprise, Harry appeared to have had a change of personality since his retirement and his late marriage to Greta. Susie was pleased by how agreeable the visit proved to be, especially as Greta was a superb baker and the afternoon tea provided was much to Susie's liking in spite of all her good resolutions about diets.

It wasn't until they were midway through the visit, with Susie savouring a second slice of chocolate cake that the conversation took an unexpected turn.

It was Alison who asked the question that set her mind racing. 'Are you from Bute, Greta, or like Harry, someone who has fallen in love with the island and decided to retire here?'

Before Greta had the opportunity to reply, Harry butted in with a note of pride in his voice. 'More than that. Greta was not only born on Bute –

she belongs to one of the oldest families on the island - the MacThreaves.'

Susie felt a sudden jolt of excitement, but unwilling to cause alarm, she continued to concentrate on eating cake, trying to appear as if she was paying little attention to this latest piece of information. Inwardly she was going over all the possibilities.

Greta might be the very person who could help her find out more about the ownership of Ettrick House. She would have to tread carefully: she'd the impression Greta was the kind of person who gave little away. So when Alison said,

'Do you know Ettrick House?' Susie could have hugged her. Greta would surely have to respond to this direct question.

Greta did reply, but in few words. 'I spent much of my childhood there.'

'In what way exactly was your family connected to the Ainslees?' One thing about Alison, thought Susie, once set on a course of action, she was like a dog with a bone.

There was a moment's hesitation, or perhaps Susie imagined it, before Greta said in such a low voice that Susie had to strain to hear, 'My family worked on the estate for many years.'

Susie was aware of Alison looking in her direction, trying to catch her eye, but she wasn't going to become involved before she'd thought through what she could add at this stage. She might say something she would later regret and more than anything she didn't want Greta to start questioning her about the inheritance. She knew so little herself.

Fortunately Greta continued without prompting, 'Yes, I knew the place well, but that was long ago. I left the island, I thought for good. But how strange life is, isn't it? Harry and I came back for a holiday and, well, the rest is, as they say, history. Unlike life in the city, life here is so easy-going.'

Alison appeared reluctant to let the subject of the Ainslees drop. 'So who were the Ainslees exactly?'

Greta sipped her tea, but said nothing and then when Susie thought she might have to say something, anything, to break the silence; it was Harry who offered some explanation. 'I've done a bit of digging – I was a history teacher, remember.'

Susie grimaced, recollecting how long-winded he could be when he got on to a favourite historical topic, but marriage had also seemed to make him less verbose.

'The Ainslees had a business in Glasgow in the 1850s. He made a fortune and had the place at Ettrick Bay built. I'm sure it was originally called after the owner. Ainslee House – yes, that's what it was.'

Greta took up the story to end with, 'The original owner William and his wife retired down here and then his son, Robert, inherited.'

Susie listened intently as the narrative of the Ainslees unfolded, all the while being careful not to look directly at Alison. So Robert Ainslee had indeed been the owner of Ettrick House originally, had left it to Robert Fraser before she inherited it? But why?

Then Harry said, quite unexpectedly, 'Greta's mother worked at Ettrick House, as did her mother before her. They...'

A look from Greta silenced him and he fumbled with his napkin to cover his embarrassment as the topic was dropped. Here was another puzzle, thought Susie.

'The house was closed up, left empty for years.' Greta made it clear this was the end of the conversation, but Susie tried to work through the implications of what she'd heard. The only possibility was that the house had proved too big to maintain and the lodge had been used as their home.

More tea and some general conversation spun out another half hour. Susie contributed little, yawning a few times in a deliberate way so that eventually Alison stood up and said, 'I think we should head back,' an opportunity Susie immediately seized.

Once in the car, Alison turned to Susie, saying, 'What do you make of Greta's story?'

Susie shrugged. She'd no intention of discussing the visit with Alison, except in general terms. There was too much information to process, too many questions remaining. If only she could find a way to talk to Greta on her own. But that would be difficult. Better to try the lawyer first and consider using Greta as a last resort. There was something disconcerting about Greta, something she couldn't put her finger on.

So all she said was, 'I'm the rightful heir. I'm going to sell it. I have to go back to the States soon anyway. The school authorities have been very good to me, but I must see out the contract.'

Alison didn't appear to be satisfied with this response, judging by the way she pursed her lips and switched on the ignition without another word.

Susie sat back. It was true she had to go back to America. This trip was no more than a mid-term break. The romance with Howard was dead, but she couldn't stop thinking about him and was still undecided about her future. The American lifestyle was appealing – not to mention the weather - but there was much she wanted to find out about Ettrick House.

What's more, she knew Alison wouldn't be able to resist pursuing the subject, and Susie had no inclination at the moment to persuade her otherwise. On her own she was having little success in her investigations.

What was it she wanted to find out? She'd no interest in the history of the Ainslees, nor in the grand Victorian mansion she'd been left, not really.

But she was interested in finding out what the relationship had been between her uncle and the man who had been the custodian of Ettrick House. Only then could she begin to move on with her life.

CHAPTER ELEVEN

Once back in the quiet of her bedroom at Ettrick House, Susie tried to absorb what she'd learned from the visit to Harry and Greta. Although her concern was with her own family, the story of the Ainslee family would have to be investigated if she was to find out the truth.

If that sort of property had been in the family her mother would surely have said something, expected the rich relatives to help out more than merely having Susie to stay for the holidays. And the lodge house wasn't exactly palatial accommodation.

Meanwhile there loomed the prospect of returning to America and dealing with the problem of Howard. Avoiding him would be impossible. They moved in the same circles, had friends in common. She'd have to think of a strategy. The easiest answer of course would be to find someone to replace Howard, but that was easier said than done.

She left Ettrick House with a promise to Alison. 'I'll keep in touch and let you know what I intend to do about selling the place,' she said, hoping her studied casual attitude would disguise what she really felt about the inheritance. She had this lurking feeling Alison was as interested in the mystery as she was and would take the opportunity to conduct an extensive investigation as soon as Susie was out of the way.

It wasn't that she didn't trust her friend, but this was something she wanted to sort out for herself. It was her own fault. If she hadn't asked Alison for help in the beginning, if she hadn't been too involved with Howard, if only, if only… Enough, she said to herself. It's too late now. You'll have to sort this out somehow.

A stopover in Glasgow was called for before she made the journey back to America. Fortunately the flat in Glasgow was between lets. The exchange visit was for one year and a friend had not only offered to take over the flat for the first six months, but had managed to find a colleague who was waiting for a new house to be built out at Buchlyvie and delighted to have a place to stay short-term.

Susie double-checked. 'Are you sure Elena doesn't move in till next week?'

On being reassured that was correct, she headed for the flat at Anniesland as soon as she reached Glasgow, lucky enough to find a taxi at the rank outside Central Station. If she did return, the purchase of a new car would be one of her first actions.

As she opened the door, a faint smell of lavender greeted her. On the hall table stood a perfume diffuser lightly scenting the air and a new, gaily coloured rug lay on the wooden floor. Good to see the tenant had been taking care of the flat, she thought.

She went through to the kitchen in the hope of making coffee, and breathed a sigh of relief as she spied the large jar sitting on the counter top. It was instant, but it was better than nothing.

Mug in hand, she went through to the tiny room at the front she used as a study. How strange it was coming back after some time away, how you saw what had been long familiar with fresh eyes. Her flat in a converted Art Deco cinema hadn't been cheap and it was one of the smallest available in the building, but it was well equipped.

'I could never live in an old house like yours, Alison,' she'd in some horror when Alison had mentioned there was a house for sale in her area. 'Far too much work, not to mention the draughts you can never seem to stop up.'

The look on her friend's face told her this had not been the most tactful of remarks and she'd hastily backtracked with, 'But of course a flat suits my lifestyle better.'

But now, returning after some months, she noticed there was work to be done – the scuffed woodwork, the grubby tiles at the bathroom sink. She grimaced. This wasn't something to worry about at the moment. Plenty of time to sort out these problems when she came back – if she came back. Howard's face flashed into mind and she firmly dismissed it as she unlocked the cupboard in the far corner of the study.

This was where she kept personal items while the flat was let, including 'bits and pieces to be sorted out' at some indeterminate date and as she opened the door, several items fell to the floor with a loud clatter. She bent to scoop them up, muttering to herself. How would she ever find what she was looking for? And yet she was sure that among these items, stacked higgedly-piggedly on top of one another, were old photo albums that might give a clue to the information she needed if she was ever to make sense of her inheritance.

She began to take everything off the shelves slowly, unwilling to risk another crash, before realising there might be a better way and went into the main bedroom to look for a cardboard box or two.

Then she remembered. The other locked cupboard in the main bedroom had a pile of flat pack boxes she'd bought some time ago to help sort out her belongings, but never got round to making up.

She pulled them out and carried them back to the study where she started two piles. One would be for possessions she wanted to keep, the second for items she could easily dispose of.

An hour later, Susie had made little progress, finding herself easily distracted by the large amount of memorabilia the cupboard contained as the mug of coffee beside her cooled untouched.

She sat back with a sigh. This was hopeless. She was looking for evidence, reminders of her early days when she went on holiday to the lodge house, not these later school photos, exercise books, birthday cards, assorted theatre programmes and old love letters.

She began to work more quickly, conscious of time passing and then on the topmost shelf she at last found the old photo album that had come from her mother's house, one of the few items she'd kept.

She pulled it down with trembling fingers and wiped the faded leather cover with a tissue she found in her pocket. She could feel her heart beating faster and faster. She couldn't remember the last time she'd looked through this, if at all, but now it would surely give her some clue to the mystery that was so perplexing her.

CHAPTER TWELVE

The first few pages were uninspiring, or at least no help in solving the puzzle: photos of her parents in the early days of their marriage. There they were on holiday on Bute, with an occasional trip south to Whitley Bay, judging by the scrawled notes on the back.

Behind those were photos of her as a baby with her parents, her father holding her, standing proudly in his soldier's uniform. She leafed through a succession of shots taken with her grandparents; several with people whose faces she didn't recognise, but could only assume were friends.

There appeared to be a gap of some time because when she next featured in the album she looked to be about six or seven years old, and after a few random photos, the album petered out to blank pages. She sat back, trying to come to terms with the feeling of disappointment. How could she have thought it would be otherwise? In the aftermath of her father's death, the last thing her mother would have been interested in was taking photos. And once her mother remarried, she wouldn't be inclined to keep anything that would remind Walter of her previous husband. That this album had survived was probably a bit of luck, no more.

She leafed through it again, but this time she paused, noticing on one of the pages the tell-tale signs of photos having been roughly torn out. There could have been any number of reasons for this, none of them sinister.

Unable to find a ladder, she went through to the kitchen and brought back one of the chairs. Climbing on to it cautiously, she couldn't quite see into the topmost shelf, but she was close enough to feel along it right to the back and to her disappointment, there were no photos there. She came down carefully. If any photos had been removed from the album, someone had done so deliberately – they hadn't fallen out.

She stood for a moment, contemplating her discovery, wondering if there was any evidence she'd missed, before suddenly noticing it had grown dark outside. She planned to stay overnight, but no more, as her flight for America left early next morning from Glasgow Airport. Aware of pangs of hunger, she went through to the kitchen, but while there was plenty of coffee, the cupboards and the fridge were bare of food. Looked like it would have to be a takeaway from the shop on the corner.

Susie bundled the whole lot back into the cupboard, stacking everything as best she could on top of the boxes. Final decisions would have to wait. In her frustrated mood she wasn't ready to sort out what she should keep and what to throw out.

As she lifted the last bag an envelope fell out and as she stooped to pick it up, to her surprise she realised the elastic band around it held together several sets of photos. She was about to pack them up with everything else she was cramming into the cupboard but then, with little hope, she sat down again to have a quick look through. There would be no harm in seeing what was here and they could then go into the appropriate box.

First impressions weren't helpful. Photos were still a rarity at the time these had been taken. She well remembered the box Brownie camera, the need to pose perfectly still, and the excitement of going to the chemist to collect the slightly out-of-focus snaps that usually took at least a week to develop.

Several were of family gatherings in Glasgow with her grandparents, though she recalled them only vaguely. In the first bundle she came across the photo of her father that had sat in the ornate frame on the mantelpiece and for a moment felt tears rise as she gazed at it.

She began to thumb through the remaining photos with few expectations. If there were any snaps taken of her holidays surely they would have been left with her relatives on the island.

Among these last few there were photos of Bute and with mounting excitement, she realised they might be what she was looking for. Clearly her mother had kept them, but not on display.

There she was, clutching a large teddy, standing at the front door of the lodge house, squinting her eyes up against the sun. The slightly out-of-focus black and white photo couldn't disguise her pleasure. That's what she remembered – the delight at being on Bute with her aunt and uncle.

There were no more than ten in total, some so blurred as to be almost unrecognizable. Whoever had taken them hadn't been particularly skilful.

Oh, there was one of her with her aunt, whose frown made her look stern, though in real life she was nothing of the kind. And one with her uncle, beaming broadly, exactly as she remembered him. All very interesting, but nothing to take her any further forward in her quest to find out about her inheritance.

At the bottom of the pile she finally discovered something that might be of use. In this one she was standing between her uncle and a man she didn't recognise. He was tall and broad, his features difficult to make out because of the large bushy beard and moustache he sported, but the overall impression was of someone very much in charge.

Who on earth was he? It wasn't her father, because this seemed to be one of the last holidays she'd had on the island, judging by her age. And it wasn't Walter: clean-shaven to the point of obsession, he wouldn't have dreamt of growing so much facial hair.

She examined the photo again, back and front, but there was no clue as to the identity of this strange man. She racked her brains, trying to recollect the photo being taken. Surely she would have remembered someone so distinguished looking. Besides, there were few visitors to the Lodge House – the milkman on his horse and cart and the postman, of course, but others were few and far between. This man certainly wasn't one of them and no one else came to mind.

By the way both men were standing, it was clear they were at ease with one another, so it must have been someone who knew her aunt and uncle well. Of that at least she was certain. She turned it over. There were initials on the back, but they were so faded as to be of little help. 'R and SR EHL' followed by an indecipherable date.

She stood up, stretching to ease her aching shoulders and scrabbled among the pile for a piece of paper and a pen. She wrote the initials down, changing them this way and that, trying to decide what they meant but after ten minutes the best she could come up with was Ettrick House Lodge for the EHL.

She went through the rest of the photos slowly, one by one, but the mystery man made no further appearances. She put the photo to one side, convinced it was the clue she'd been looking for. But the clue to what, she had no idea.

CHAPTER THIRTEEN

Susie slept badly and when she did doze off, it was to dream of the lodge house where the man with the fine set of whiskers seemed to be chasing her up and down the dusty road.

When the alarm went off in the early hours of the morning it was a few moments before she realised where she was. Suppressing the desire to snuggle back down under the duvet for another half hour, she slid out of bed and made her way to the kitchen to reach for the jar of coffee almost on automatic pilot.

Fortunately she hadn't brought much luggage back with her, so packing wouldn't take long, though she added a couple of items from her wardrobe in the flat that might be useful in the kinder climate of Los Angeles.

The last thing she slipped into her bag was the photo, hoping that if she looked at it often enough she might jolt her memory. She rinsed out her coffee mug, gathered her belongings and with a last quick check round the flat, locked up and headed down in the lift to the waiting taxi she'd ordered the night before.

As they sped through the Clyde tunnel towards the motorway leading to the airport, Susie felt her concerns receding. What did it matter why she'd been left this massive house on Bute? There was no way she could realistically keep it, could afford to maintain something of that size, no matter how nostalgic she might feel about it. The extent of the decay, the building work needed both inside and out were beyond her means – and her strength. It was doubtful if she could even manage to continue as the owner of the lodge house. After all, in spite of the end of her romance with Howard, she might decide to stay in the States in which case a holiday home on Bute would be a foolish indulgence.

With her mind made up, she looked more positively towards her future in the States. It might not have worked out with Howard, but life in America held other attractions.

Susie had carefully avoided contact with Alison, except for the odd text, telling herself she was too busy for a lengthy phone call, grateful as she was for her friend's ongoing support. Anyway, she reassured herself, trying to dismiss the pangs of guilt about her lack of communication, Alison and Simon loved Bute, would surely be enjoying their time on the island.

She'd the distinct feeling Alison was anxious to tempt her to return to Scotland and at the moment this was the last thing she wanted, not until she was certain of the story behind her inheritance and how her future might be if she managed to remain in America.

Once back in Los Angeles, she'd slid easily into the casual lifestyle, made new friends, overcome any angst about Howard who, she'd heard, had changed jobs and moved with his family to Indiana. It might or might not have been to do with her, but whatever the reason, there was little doubt it was convenient. Trouble was, it might take some time before she could forget him completely.

After postponing a reply several times, there was finally no option: she had to respond to Alison's calls. Alison might try to prevail on her, but Susie was determined her decision wasn't about to be overturned.

Even Alison's pleas, 'You're needed back at Strathelder. We've two staff off on long-term sick leave, one on maternity leave and your replacement clearly can't cope with the Scottish system,' didn't change her decision.

'I guess the Head thinks you might have more success at persuading me than she did,' was Susie's reply. 'Sorry, but I have a contract here and I have to remind you this is an exchange visit.'

Alison didn't reply, confirming the impression Susie had gained that her American counterpart wasn't as entranced by Scotland as she was by America.

'But surely you'll want to come back to Ettrick House. I know it needs a lot of work, but plenty of people would be delighted to inherit a property like this...'

Susie cut in, 'I can't possibly live there, not now, not ever. I am grateful to you, but I could never afford the upkeep. It needs far too much work. I want the place sold. I'll sort it all out as soon as I can.'

'But...' said Alison.

'Any more word on the skeleton?' said Susie, changing the subject to one she knew would be absorbing her friend's interest.

Her guess had been correct. 'No more word yet, Susie, except that it's been confirmed it's Roman. The archaeologists are very excited, but they're keeping the details quiet at the moment. They've organised a Press conference so we should learn more shortly.' There was a pause.

'So how are you? Are you managing okay?'

Susie smiled, knowing Alison was really asking if she was over her relationship with Howard.

'I'm fine, honestly. There's no need to worry.'

Now was the time to tell Alison of her plans, thought Susie, saying, 'I'm going to instruct an estate agent to put the house on the market.'

'Do you think that's wise? Wouldn't you be better to wait till this whole business is cleared up?'

'Why? It might take ages for that to happen. And meanwhile I'm responsible for the bills.'

'It's your choice.' There was a frosty note in Alison's reply. Surely she wasn't becoming so enchanted by Ettrick House that she wanted it for herself, thought Susie?

'Can you possibly help, Alison? Being so far away means it's difficult to make arrangements.'

'You'll have to come home at some point. We don't own the property and I don't think they would take our word for it that you want to sell it.

Remember the difficulties we had in the beginning when you asked us to look after the house.'

'I might manage over for a few days,' said Susie, suspecting a week would be the minimum necessary to start proceedings before she could leave Alison to continue with the sale.

Truth was, she'd had enough of her inheritance. All she wanted to do now was finish with Ettrick House. Despite its current state and with the market as sluggish as it was, it should fetch a fair amount of money. Perhaps a developer would take it on. Even someone with an unusually large family would find its cavernous rooms too much.

'And in the meantime, will you continue to keep an eye on it? There's no one else I can rely on.'

Susie heard Alison's deep sigh. 'Yes, Susie, I suppose we can do that. The May holiday is coming up – we can go over then. It's probably a good idea to keep tabs on the archaeologists anyway. Goodness knows what they might have uncovered in the grounds.'

Susie put the phone down with mixed feelings of relief and of guilt, well aware that without Alison's help everything would have been much trickier, if not impossible.

She'd a lesson to prepare for the next day, something to engage the students' interest. Though there was much about the lifestyle she enjoyed, the students at Thomas Paine were far more demanding than the students at Strathelder High and only too ready to let you know if they were finding your lesson boring.

Before beginning she pulled out the photo of her uncle with the unidentified man, propping it on the table by the window. There must be some way of finding out who was the man in the photo other than hoping she would suddenly remember.

It would be just her luck if he turned out to be someone of no consequence, but she had this strange feeling that wasn't the case. He must be somebody her relatives had known well, else why photograph him with her uncle in the days when so few photos were taken?

She stared at the photo until she felt a headache coming on. As in a flash, an idea came to her, left her wondering why she hadn't thought of this sooner. There was only one person it could be - Robert Fraser.

Could she check out information about Ettrick House on the internet? She'd used it for some research to do with the topics she'd prepared for school, so surely there must be information somewhere about the people who had lived at Ettrick House. She tried to remember exactly what Greta had said that afternoon she and Alison had visited.

All thought of lesson preparation forgotten, she rummaged for a notepad and pencil and sat down to make a list of all the questions she hoped she'd finally be able to answer.

CHAPTER FOURTEEN

Finding the answers wasn't as easy as she'd anticipated. While there was plenty of information about Bute on the internet and even several mentions of Ettrick House, there was little of any use about the Ainslee family beyond the sketchy information Greta had provided.

A phone call from Alison seemed more promising: she had been doing some investigation in the local library in Rothesay, using the back copies of the local paper, The Buteman.

'William Ainslee built the house. He had one sister Beatrice, but she seems to have decided going back to Glasgow was better than life on the island. His son was Robert, but he died without an heir, so as you said there must be a family connection between the Ainslees and your mother.'

'That's all very interesting, Alison, but it doesn't take me much further forward with finding out about this Robert Fraser, though it is a coincidence he had the same name as my uncle. I need to find out what was the relationship – there must have been one if Robert Ainslee left Ettrick House in the care of Mr. Fraser.'

'If they had the same name perhaps that was the key,' suggested Alison.

'Oh, for goodness sake, that's no reason to leave a mansion to someone because you shared the same name. I'm assuming he was an employee. Perhaps it was a reward for long and faithful service.'

From her next words it was clear Alison thought it prudent to change the subject. 'So you've definitely decided to sell up?'

'Of course. I haven't learned anything that would make me change my mind. I'm going to book a short trip back to sort out an estate agent and then once it's on the market they can handle the work connected with selling.' A pause, then she added, 'You and Simon have done more than enough to help. I do appreciate it. Not unless you'd like to buy it?'

The laugh accompanying this remark was intended to reassure Alison Susie was only joking but even so the reply came in no uncertain terms, 'Absolutely not,' before adding, 'but you might be here for the archaeologists' Press conference. It promises to be exciting.'

'I wouldn't miss it,' said Susie before ringing off. She sat for a while, digesting what Alison had said, before going back to her computer. Surely with this additional information she might be able to untangle the strange bond between her relatives and the Frasers.

Lifting the photo she'd brought with her from Scotland, she sat frowning at it, hoping for inspiration, but still came up with the same answer. The man in the photo could only be Robert Fraser.

She examined the details of the clothing carefully, hoping to find some clue, but there was nothing to help her.

She tried to reassess the information she'd gleaned so far, thinking how much easier it would have been had she asked her mother about her family. Somehow it was a subject never discussed.

Opening her notepad, she began to write down everything she could remember about her mother's family, but there was very little and when it was finished she stared at the few facts she'd managed to marshal. Sure, it told her a chronological story, but that was all. It took her no further forward.

Perhaps there was someone in her father's family who might help? It would be worth a try.

Why had she been so curt with Alison, who was so much better at this kind of thing than she was? But at the moment she preferred not to let her friend know of her attempts to discover the connection. Time enough when she had some concrete information.

She packed everything away carefully, giving each item a final glance as she did so. She was booked on a flight home the following week and short as that trip would be, it might be her last opportunity to find out the truth about her inheritance before there were new owners of the Victorian mansion.

CHAPTER FIFTEEN

There was one last option Susie hadn't thought of, though whether it would prove to be a lead or another dead end she was prepared to take a gamble. A trawl of the photos had reminded her that her father had had a cousin who lived out at Drymen, not far from Glasgow.

She had a vague recollection of some story about a family fall-out, a quarrel of some kind, and though she'd never discovered the details, she was now sure it must have been to do with her mother and father's marriage.

Her father's relative had had a couple of children, but she found it impossible to remember their names or even their gender. Still, it might be worth trying to contact them and once back in her Glasgow flat and over the worst of the jet lag she headed for the local library to consult the phone books, hoping one of them might still live in the area. If that didn't help she could consult the electoral roll. She'd managed to secure leave for a whole week at home, but only because the other teachers had rallied round to help, intrigued by what little she'd told them of her situation.

'Gee,' Ethel had said, 'a mansion on an island. It's the sort of thing you read about in fairy tales. I can't believe you're being so cool about it.'

Ethel clearly had a false impression of this particular Victorian mansion, but Susie kept her own counsel. No point in destroying her illusions.

In a renewed spirit of optimism Susie set off. Through a friend's recommendation she'd managed to find an estate agent who seemed enthused by the idea of selling Ettrick House. She'd only been able to speak to him on the phone so far, but was looking forward to the appointment with him. Only then would she at last feel she was making real progress.

She decided to walk. The library wasn't far, the sun was shining and the parking at the library could be difficult. As she crossed the street she caught a glimpse of the reflection of someone who looked vaguely familiar in the nearest shop window, but when she turned to look there was no one in sight. Must have been my imagination, she thought as she continued, pondering the best way to start her search.

Assisted by a very helpful librarian, she was able to track down one of her father's relatives much more quickly than anticipated, in part because she had a sudden flash of memory about the address.

'22 Benvue Way,' she said in response to the librarian's question, astonished at where that recollection had come from. It was even more fortunate this relative was male and hadn't changed his name.

Thanking the librarian profusely, she left the library almost light-hearted. Here finally was a piece of the jigsaw that might give her a better picture.

She stopped outside the butcher's. Fine – she had a name and an address and it would be no problem now to get the phone number. But what would she say? And what if he refused to see her, put the phone down? People had so many scam calls these days and Tony must be well over seventy by now. No, better to take a chance and head out towards Drymen. At the very least she could have a snoop around, leave a note if Tony wasn't at home.

As she turned away, once more she was conscious of someone nearby, no more than the glimpse of a shadowy figure and she whirled round only to find yet again that there was no one in sight.

Get a grip, she told herself, you're imagining things. She strode purposefully back towards the flat to collect her car and head for Drymen.

With no satnav in her elderly car, Susie was relieved to find that the road out from Glasgow was well-signposted and once she reached the junction at Anniesland Cross it was a straight drive up the Bearsden Road and through Milngavie towards her destination.

She tried to concentrate on the way ahead, but the green fields, the sights and sounds of the country were distracting and it was some time before she realised she was well away from any other traffic. The route she'd looked up before leaving showed that the address wasn't in Drymen itself, but in the village of Culmach a little way out and she became increasingly nervous, aware of being out of her comfort zone, as all signs of habitation disappeared.

Rather than make a mistake and take the wrong route, Susie drew into a lay by to consult her map. Yes, she was indeed on the right road. This wasn't the time to give in to doubts and having come this far she was determined to continue.

She glanced in the rear view mirror. That was strange. A car had come up behind her. She hadn't noticed it at first, but now observed it had stopped a little way back in a passing place and was sitting there, its engine running.

Behave, she scolded herself. You are such a townie. Probably someone stopping to admire the scenery, unaware it was illegal to park in a passing place.

Putting any anxieties firmly to one side, she started up the engine and moved off, glancing again in her rear view mirror as she did so, only to see to her surprise that the car had pulled out behind her.

There was a way to find out if this was her imagination and she deliberately slowed to a crawl, flashing her indicator to show she was allowing the other car to overtake. There was no response and the car continued to tail her, matching her speed for speed, mile for mile.

Though not nervous by nature, Susie was beginning to feel alarmed and no matter how much she tried to tell herself she was being silly she couldn't shake off the fear that she was being followed. But by whom? And why out here?

Then she recollected the feeling she'd had on the way to and from the library, of someone just out of sight, someone she should recognise. Was it the same person who had followed her out here? What nonsense.

She increased her speed, skittering round the sudden bends and twists in the road. This was the only way to shake off the car behind and as she turned a particularly nasty bend she glanced back to see it had disappeared.

It was her imagination after all and she breathed a sigh of relief. The car must have turned off down one of the side roads or tracks, many of which led to grand country houses well concealed by high trees and dense shrubbery.

She settled back to drive more slowly, anxious not to miss the sign for Culmach. The last thing she wanted to do was drive past it and then have to find a way back, as she'd failed to spot any opportunities to turn safely.

Concentrating hard on finding the village, she didn't notice that the car had come up behind her once more and by the time she did, it was sitting close on her tail. Now more angry than afraid, she began to increase her speed, but the car following did likewise.

And now Susie took a risk. She would speed up even more and see how the driver coped with that. She pressed hard on the accelerator and gripped the steering wheel tightly. Let whoever it was see if they could catch up with her.

A few moments later there was a roar and she felt her car being shunted, once, twice. There was a sharp bend in the road ahead and before Susie could take evasive action she found herself heading for one of the large trees beside the verge.

She wrested the steering wheel round in the opposite direction as hard as she could and stamped on the brakes, but the best she could manage was to avoid the tree, only to end up in the ditch at the side of the road as the other car roared past.

She sat for a moment or two trying to gather her wits before becoming aware of a searing pain in her right arm. She tried to move it, but the pain increased and she had to accept it was probably broken.

She leaned over to the passenger seat, trying to extract her phone with her good arm, conscious with every movement of the pain in her other arm. Thank goodness she hadn't passed out, though feelings of nausea threatened to overcome her at any minute.

After three attempts she managed to dial the emergency service and, reassured they would be with her soon, she sat back, feeling the hurt wash over her, trying not to give in to the desire to faint. Whatever had been going on, of one thing she was certain. The car had been following her deliberately and had forced her to crash off the road on purpose. This was no accident.

CHAPTER SIXTEEN

As Alison and Simon came rushing into the side room in the hospital ward, Susie felt her eyes filling with tears, but she brushed them away, persuading herself they were no more than a reaction to the shock of the crash. 'Oh, Alison, am I glad to see you,' she said.

Alison was as brusque as usual, though Susie knew it was a sign of how concerned she was. 'What on earth happened to you?' she asked, leaning over to kiss her friend.

'A car accident, if you could call it that. Someone tried to run me off the road.'

Seeing the look of horror on Alison's face, Susie went on, 'I know what you're thinking, Alison, but it wasn't my stupidity. Someone deliberately tried to make me crash. I was lucky I wasn't killed.'

She lay back on the bed, exhausted by the effort of speaking and closed her eyes as one of the nurses came bustling over, saying, 'I think that's enough for the moment. She's still under sedation.'

'What's wrong with her exactly?' whispered Alison.

'Cuts and bruises and a broken arm. She'll be fine. She needs time to recover.'

'We'll sit with her for a little while,' said Alison though it was clear Susie had drifted off to sleep.

A short time later Simon, who'd elected to go down to the canteen for coffee, returned to the ward saying, 'Let's go, Alison. We can stay overnight at home and come back tomorrow.'

Reluctantly Alison agreed this would be the best course of action and with several backward glances at the sound asleep Susie, she tiptoed from the room.

Next day when Alison and Simon came back to the hospital, Susie was sitting up in bed, complaining loudly at the prospect of having to remain for a further couple of days. 'I'm fine to go home,' she kept saying to which Alison tried to persuade her otherwise saying, 'Be sensible, Susie, you've had a nasty fright.'

In spite of her protestations, Susie knew that, were she to get her way and be discharged, it would be difficult to manage on her own in her Glasgow flat.

'Tell you what,' said Alison. 'Let's go to Bute. You can convalesce there more easily.' She looked at Simon for approval, but he shook his head. 'I can't afford any more time away from college,' he said when they were out of earshot as Susie got dressed.

'Anyway,' he added, 'what about her return to the States? What is she going to do about that?'

'There's no way she can go back at present,' said Alison. 'If the worst comes to the worst, she can cut short her American Exchange and return to Strathelder.'

Simon shook his head. 'I know that would suit Strathelder, Alison, but I'm not sure Susie would agree.'

Alison ignored his doubts. 'She might have no option,' she said.

With a course of action decided, Alison and Susie headed for Bute, only stopping briefly by Susie's flat to gather some essentials.

Susie suspected there was a lot Alison wasn't saying, but she didn't have to. It was perfectly clear that whoever had run her off the road, it was no accident. Far from it. It had been a deliberate attempt if not to kill her, then at the very least to give her a fright. And the only reason she could come up with was it was something to do with the house at Ettrick Bay.

It was more important than ever for Susie to find out the terms of her inheritance.

CHAPTER SEVENTEEN

After a few days on Bute Susie felt sufficiently strong to venture out alone. Alison fretted over her like a mother hen and, grateful as she was for the concern, Susie was determined to make another visit to the lodge house. Surely it was the most likely place for her to find information about her inheritance. Last time she hadn't been thorough enough, or so she convinced herself.

She'd been reluctant to leave Glasgow without seeing Tony, but he had been so kind when she eventually phoned him. 'I'm not going anywhere,' he said. 'Give me a ring when you're back on the mainland and we can meet up. I'm always glad of an excuse to go in to Glasgow.'

She hadn't told Alison about contacting Tony and it had taken all her skills to come up with a plausible reason to explain why she had been out driving in the country. Alison's, 'Mmm,' was a sign her story, 'I fancied some fresh air and heard Drymen was worth a visit,' wasn't believed.

And now whenever she suggested going off on her own, Alison insisted on coming with her.

'It's no trouble,' she would say. 'I could do with a walk.'

On more than one occasion Susie was tempted to take Alison into her confidence, but something always held her back. It wasn't that she didn't trust her friend, but she might be on a wild goose chase and she didn't want Alison fretting over concerns about her health.

But as the days passed, albeit slowly, Susie felt her strength return, her arm healed more quickly than anticipated and on a final visit to the local Hospital in Rothesay the doctor gave her the all clear. 'Good as new,' he grinned, much to her relief.

The next afternoon, Alison declared she had to go into town. 'We're running low on tea and milk,' she said. 'Those archaeologists are a thirsty lot. Do you want to come with me?'

Susie shook her head. 'I'll be fine here.' Aware she would soon have to return to America, Susie wanted to take this opportunity to go down to the lodge house.

It was clear Alison wasn't happy leaving Susie on her own. 'The outing might do you good and we could stop off on the way back and have coffee and cake in the Ettrick Bay Tearoom.'

Even this prospect wasn't enough to tempt Susie. She had to do the search without alerting Alison and an opportunity like this might not come again any time soon.

Alison put on her coat saying, 'Promise me you'll stay here and rest. That you won't go wandering off.'

'I won't go far,' said Susie, crossing her fingers behind her back. You couldn't call a stroll down to the lodge house 'wandering off.'

'I'll be as quick as I can,' were Alison's parting words as Susie settled down on the sofa with a book she'd found in the old library, giving every appearance of planning to be there for the afternoon.

The moment she heard the sound of Alison's car starting up and roaring down the drive, Susie tossed the book aside and jumped to her feet. She felt shaky, but only briefly, and she went into her bedroom to collect the notebook where she'd written down a list of questions.

No matter what Alison thought, no matter how much danger she might be in, finding out why she had come by this inheritance would be the key to the puzzle.

She ambled down the sweeping driveway, enjoying the freshness of the air. It might be colder than Los Angeles, but there were compensations. Was she being swayed by the better climate, the relaxed lifestyle in California? Alison had said as much. 'It's always exciting working in a new place, Susie, but the attraction will wear off after a while. Mark my words.'

At the time Susie had scoffed, but now walking down the driveway, stopping for a moment as the distant bay came into view, she wasn't sure what she wanted to do. Had she been swayed by the romance (if it could be called that, she thought bitterly) with Howard?

Almost before she knew it, she turned the corner and there was the lodge house, sitting quietly in the late afternoon sunshine, looking a little worse for wear, a little scruffy and unloved. Perhaps she could sell Ettrick House and keep the lodge? That would work out well. She was sure Simon and Alison would be happy to use it from time to time and there were other friends who would be equally delighted to escape from the city. If only she could make up her mind.

She stood still, examining it again, taking in each curve and line of the building. Last time she'd been here, she'd given the place only the most cursory search. Now she was determined to find some answers. As she stood there, memories came flooding back and she could almost see her young self skipping and hopping in the front garden as the afternoon shadows lengthened before she was summoned indoors for tea.

She opened the door slowly, intending to make every moment count, use this opportunity to recall what had happened all those years ago. Somewhere in the dim recesses of her mind information must be lurking, waiting to be brought out.

This time, the place seemed even dustier than ever, though it had only been a few weeks since she'd last been there. In this old lodge, in the complete silence, whispers of those who once lived here seemed to linger.

She went through to the living room and sat on the ancient sofa, ignoring the cloud of dust that rose as she sat down with a thump. She suddenly realised she was still tired, still suffering the after effects of the accident.

She'd looked everywhere she could think of on her previous visit, now it was time to look in those places she hadn't considered.

Where would her uncle keep important information? One thing she was sure of was that it would be her uncle who would be responsible for any legal matters and surely he must have had some papers, some documents relating to the inheritance of Ettrick House.

She opened her notebook and thumbed through the pages, feeling depressed at how little information she had. Whatever the link, it had to be between the Ainslees and Robert Fraser. Could it be a blood relationship? No, that wasn't at all likely.

Family ties were so complicated, she thought. Her stepfather had been kind to her, had insisted she use his name, but had never formally adopted her, which meant it was easy to go back to using her father's name of Littlejohn when she became adult.

She stood up. This wasn't getting her any further forward, sitting dreaming like this.

She went over to the large dresser that sat against the wall, opening the cupboards and the drawers in a desultory fashion, telling herself it was a waste of time as she'd gone through it all on her last visit.

She examined the bookshelves. Not that her aunt and uncle had been great readers, but there was the obligatory large family Bible, the copies of Dickens' Pickwick Papers, a collection of books about the wildlife of Bute and a few romantic paperbacks which must have belonged to her aunt.

She wandered into the kitchen, opening drawers and cupboards. She found some black bin bags and began to empty the various packets and tins of food into them. She was in no mood to consider sell by dates. It all had to go. She would have to make a start on the china, the pots and pans and all the rest of the kitchen equipment, but she lacked the energy for that task at the moment.

After stacking the several bags she'd filled beside the front door, she realised she'd have to find out which day the bins were collected.

Upstairs her aunt and uncle's room was as spartan as the rest of the house: a large bed, a cupboard on either side, a wardrobe they'd evidently shared judging by the collection of clothes. Something else to organise, dispose of. It would be so much easier to engage a house clearing firm but she would feel a certain disloyalty in doing that.

It was hopeless: there was nothing here, no evidence. Yet it was so unlike her organised uncle to leave no trace, no information. It was hard to believe the owner of a house like Ettrick would be living in this way.

As she went slowly downstairs, a yawning tiredness crept over her. It would take all her energy to go back up the driveway to the main house and flop on the sofa.

She peeked in for a last time at the living room, more and more aware that house clearance firm would be the only solution, in spite of her scruples.

As she made to turn away, to leave the house, her eye was caught by the bookshelves. Perhaps it was the angle she was now viewing them from, but one book stood out from the others by its size and its thick leather cover. The family Bible. A memory came flooding back, of her uncle sitting by the fire, lit against the unexpected chill of a summer's evening, saying to her, 'All the best stories are in here, Susie. Make sure you remember that. You don't have to look anywhere else for inspiration.'

At the time she'd paid no heed. She was only a child and assumed he meant the stories of Ruth and Moses and Noah, but supposing he'd meant something else? Had been giving her an indication as to where he kept important papers?

She crossed the room and pulled the Bible from the shelf, almost losing her balance as she staggered under the weight. She sat back down on the sofa and opened it, hoping that at last she might have found some of the answers she was seeking.

CHAPTER EIGHTEEN

The Bible was heavy and after several attempts to manage its unwieldy size on her lap, Susie pulled over the side table, moving the lamp on to the floor to create more room. She leaned forward and opened the book carefully, conscious of its delicate state. Immediately behind the ornate frontispiece, gilded and in an ancient script, were several pages available for inserting important family dates and there, filled out in her aunt's spidery handwriting were details of the births, marriages and deaths of what were clearly members of the family.

She examined each of the entries carefully, aware of surprise after surprise as she read the names of people she'd no idea existed: second cousins, great aunts and uncles she'd never heard mentioned. What's more, they all seemed to be related to the Frasers. This Bible couldn't be

Robert Ainslee's - it must have belonged to Robert Fraser, because nowhere was there a mention of any of the Ainslees. The only explanation she could think of was that Robert Fraser had lived in the lodge house after her aunt and uncle died.

She reread the entries, frowning in bewilderment. This was all very interesting, but it wasn't helping. She scrabbled in her bag for a pen and a piece of paper, but all she could find was an old receipt. She stood up, stretching to ease the crick in her neck. There must be something she could write on, put the details from the Bible in some kind of order. Surely that would help her understand.

After looking through several drawers she finally found a notepad in the sideboard. The paper was very flimsy, but it would have to do. Carefully she transcribed the details, taking note of dates, highlighting those she was unsure about. But after almost an hour working, all she had was a family tree of sorts and nowhere in any of the pages was there the slightest sign that any of them, even the most distant, had been connected to the Ainslee family. It was as great a puzzle as ever.

Perhaps she should stop investigating the past, trying to find out why she had been left Ettrick House, and concentrate on her future. Why did any of it matter? She should sell up, yes even this little lodge house, and use the money to buy a house more suited to her needs. But where would that house be? Glasgow or Los Angeles? This was hopeless. She was going round and round in circles.

She began to turn the pages of the Bible idly. How long was it since she'd read one? Not for years. Once again she recalled her uncle sitting by the fire, his Bible open in front of him. Again she could almost hear him saying, 'All the best stories are to be found here...'

Had she been mistaken? Was that what he'd said? Probably her uncle had been doing no more than professing his belief that here could be found words of wisdom by which to run your life. In her desperation for a solution she was making something out of nothing.

She reached the Book of Job and was about to close the Bible, restore it to its place on the shelf, when she caught a glimpse of a thin piece of paper fluttering to the ground. She bent to retrieve it, carefully unfolding it as she did so.

The handwriting was faded and in places indecipherable, but what was clear was the heading at the top: 'Bilson and Sons, Solicitors and Notaries' followed by an address in St Vincent Street in Glasgow.

She felt her pulse quicken. Surely here was some information of a legal kind, but as she looked closer she saw it was in the form of a letter.

'Dear Sir,

Further to our recent correspondence with Mr. Robert Ainslee, owner of Ettrick House, Ettrick Bay, Isle of Bute I can confirm we will be proceeding in accordance with his instructions of the 15th inst.'

This was followed by several lines where the letter had been folded over and was so creased only the odd word could be deciphered, no matter how much she twisted the paper this way and that.

Giving up any further attempt she looked at the bottom of the page where she could make out '....signature verified...' 'your agreement to the conditions as specified in...' and then a few faded words until the letter ended

'...and assuring you at all times of our best attention...' followed by a very blurred signature which she could only assume was one of the Bilsons.

She stood up and went over to the window to hold the paper up to the light, but that made it no clearer. Were Bilson and Sons still in operation? Unable to make out the date of the letter, she realised it could have been written at any point in her uncle's life. Was this something to do with the inheritance? What were the conditions and what were they referring to? She felt as though she was creeping tantalizingly close, only to have her hopes crushed.

She would take this letter with her and try to find the Bilson firm or someone who might have taken them over. She now had an address and as their office had been in St Vincent Street in Glasgow near the George Square end, the building would still be there.

About to heave the book back on to its rightful place on the shelf, she hesitated for a moment. Best to double check there wasn't anything else of interest. So thin was the paper of this letter she'd almost missed it. It looked as if her uncle used the Bible as the safest place to keep important documents.

A further careful trawl through the pages and she was in luck. Sandwiched between the last pages was a scrap of paper, with the appearance of having been torn from another letter, and as she read it, Susie realised this one added a whole new dimension to the story.

If her guess was correct, this might explain why Robert Ainslee had left the house to Robert Fraser. Or was she engaging in wild speculation in her increasing anxiety to find answers?

CHAPTER NINETEEN

Susie had to think of a pretext for going back to Glasgow, something that would satisfy Alison who was still expressing concerns about Susie's recovery.

If she could first track information about the Bilson firm, that might help also her find out more about the strange scrap of letter she'd found.

'I can manage perfectly all right on my own,' she replied to Alison's, 'I'm happy to come back with you, help you get whatever you need from your flat. Though I thought,' she added sharply, 'you said you'd brought enough to be going on with for your time here.'

'It's my correspondence about the post in America,' said Susie, suddenly inspired by what she hoped was a credible reason.

'Couldn't you tell me where the papers are and Simon could collect them and bring them down at the weekend?' She frowned.

Susie stood her ground, determined not to give in to Alison's concerns. 'No, it's not as simple as that. I need to look through them, find the ones that I need. It's a job I have to do myself.'

'Okay,' said Alison grudgingly, 'but I will come with you. There are a couple of things I have to attend to in Glasgow so it'll be a good opportunity.'

With that Susie had to be content, knowing Alison could be every bit as stubborn as she was, but she was more determined than ever to have time on her own to pursue Bilson and Sons or whichever firm had taken over from them. Perhaps something would occur to her on the journey back to Glasgow. She certainly hoped so.

It was with some difficulty she persuaded Alison to, 'go off and do what you have to. I'll be fine to manage home,' as soon as they arrived at Central Station, having decided to leave the car on

Bute. Susie had the distinct impression this decision was to make sure they went back. Alison was taking the business of Susie's recuperation very seriously.

Once she made sure Alison was on her way to the suburban train line, Susie said, 'I'll go over to the Cashline and then buy a paper before I go home.' Instead she headed out of the station by the main entrance and walked towards St Vincent Street.

Though she hadn't been away from Glasgow for long, after the peace of Bute and the absolute quiet of Ettrick Bay, the noise and the bustle of the city came as a shock. She had forgotten how quickly everyone moved, jostling and pushing, crossing against red lights with a casualness that infuriated drivers. Perhaps a life on Bute was a good option after all. She was wrong - she should sell the Glasgow flat and keep the lodge house.

With every step she took, she became more and more convinced of the foolishness of this venture. There had been no date on the letter, but judging by the style of writing and the state of the paper, it hadn't been written any time recently. The likelihood of finding Bilson and Sons still in operation was more than remote.

She glanced at her watch. Plenty of time before the meeting she'd arranged with Tony to start the search for the lawyer's office. She headed for one of the cafes on Buchanan Street and over a large cappuccino debated what to do. Was this a waste of time? Even the likelihood of someone remembering Bilson and Sons was a vain hope. It would be easier forget this quest, to head for the Buchanan Galleries and do some shopping until it was time to meet up with Alison again or take a taxi to her flat as she'd proposed.

As she drained the last of her coffee she had to acknowledge her curiosity would never be satisfied if she backed out now, and standing up with a renewed sense of determination, she headed for George Square. She had an hour in hand before meeting Tony Littlejohn in the café at John Lewis.

At the first intersection she turned right into St Vincent Place and began to walk along slowly, examining the numbers closely. Yes, this was certainly the right area. The tall red sandstone buildings loomed over her, their windows ornately carved, topped by gigantic statues of various mythological creatures she couldn't identify, a testament to the skill of Victorian craftsmen in a way that wouldn't be possible in the construction of a modern office block.

The problem was where to start. Scrutinising each nameplate as she passed, eventually she reached the junction of Queen Street and St Vincent Place. She stood looking back down the length of the street, completely at a loss what to do next. She'd agreed with Alison that she'd be back at Central Station for the three fifty train to Wemyss Bay and she had to get to her flat to collect enough bits and pieces to allay her friend's suspicions about the true purpose of this trip.

There was only one thing for it. She'd have to choose one of the buildings, go in and ask. She retraced her steps, carefully examining each entrance, finally opting for one where several highly polished brass nameplates adorned the main door.

The ground floor was occupied by a firm of travel agents and Susie bustled forward, intending to make it clear to the very young, very blonde girl sitting behind the desk that she wasn't a customer.

'I know this is a long shot,' she said, 'but I'm looking for a firm of solicitors who used to be here – Bilson and Sons.'

The girl looked up from her computer screen. 'Sorry, I think you have the wrong place. This is a Travel Agency. Are you certain it was here?'

Susie shook her head, setting her dangling silver earrings dancing. 'No, I'm not even sure it was this building. All I know is that they operated out of an office in St Vincent Street many years ago.'

The girl frowned and glanced around as though seeking help from a colleague, but everyone was busy with customers. 'I can't help you, I'm sorry,' she said briskly, dismissing Susie and turning back to her computer screen.

This was a waste of time, thought Susie as she left. How long would it take her to check out all the companies in this street and in the end it might be for nothing.

Dejected by her first attempt, she left, crossed the road and stood gazing up at the soaring columns and flutes of the next building. She was about to turn away when something caught her eye. It was very faint, no more than the ghost of an outline, but on the window of the third floor of what was now a shipping line, there were the letters Bilson and...The remainder was faded, but this was enough to set her heart racing.

She crossed back to hurry up the steps. To her surprise and delight the interior of this building appeared to have changed little. Inside the close, tiled in ornate green glazed tiles, a set of well worn steps led to the various floors, the banisters of wood and highly polished brass. On the right side of the entrance a series of old-fashioned post boxes sat, each company identified by a brass plate with the name etched in black.

Susie scanned these eagerly then sighed with disappointment. Of course it had been too much to hope that Bilson and Sons might still have an office here. Even so, there was some trace of them.

She began to count the boxes, trying to align them with the office the solicitors had once occupied. Yes, there it was. Third floor, first on the right.

She headed for the lift, then stopped. This was another feature that hadn't been updated. In front of her was what looked like the original lift, its metal gates shut fast on a polished wooden structure that looked decidedly insecure. But what was the alternative? There were a great many steep stairs between the ground and the third floor and reluctantly she pressed the bell to open the gates. She pulled the metal gates over to close them, selected the button for the third floor and squeezed her eyes tight shut as the lift clattered and creaked its way upwards to stop with a loud bump at her destination.

The office she'd suspected of being the one-time premises of Bilton and Sons now proclaimed itself as Party Events for All and she did as the large notice on the door bade her.

'Don't knock, come right in.'

The office itself was like a party venue: bright streamers and banners offering Happy Birthday or Congratulations or Love to the New Arrival adorned every corner, complemented by balloons of all sizes and colours. The girl sitting in the chair in the far corner was equally colourful with pink and mauve streaked hair and several studs in each ear, all set off by an assortment of clothes that looked to have been selected at random. Susie felt dull in comparison.

She explained what she wanted, with little hope of success. If Bilson and Sons had once occupied these premises, even their ghosts would have vanished by now under this onslaught of modern entertainment.

But to her great surprise the girl said in reply to her question, 'Oh, you'll want to talk to Freddie. When he took this place over it was in a terrible state with all the old filing cabinets and stuff still here.'

She stood up and crossed to the door in the corner. 'Freddie,' she called, 'here's a woman wanting to know about the office you took over.'

Freddie appeared, his gnome-like appearance contrasting sharply with that of his assistant.

'How can I help you?'

Once again Susie explained the purpose of her visit. It was unlikely that this company would have preserved the archives of Bilson and Sons. But once again she was proved wrong.

'Ah, yes,' said Freddie, pursing his lips and making his hands into a steeple as children do. 'There was so much stuff everywhere – in filing cabinets, in boxes, in drawers.' He shuddered. 'Lots of old paper.'

'So you got rid of everything?'

Freddie's eyes widened in astonishment. 'Of course not. It might have been valuable. We had no way of knowing. This office had lain empty for years and years. I believe the Bilson family owned the lease until the eighties and weren't prepared to relet the place. Probably nowhere else to put everything, all that legal stuff.'

'So what did you do with it?' asked Susie, conscious of the minutes ticking past.

'Oh, someone from the Bilson family came and took it away. Well, I insisted. There was no way I wanted to be left with the responsibility, did I?'

Another dead end, thought Susie, then she said, 'Well, thanks for your time,' and turned to go.

'Wait,' said Freddie, catching her by the arm. 'Don't you want their address, if you are so interested in them?'

'You have their address?' Susie couldn't disguise her astonishment.

'Of course.' Freddie drew himself up. 'There was SO much stuff. I wanted to make sure EVERY scrap of it went. Wait a minute.'

He disappeared into the back shop and Susie heard him rummaging about, opening and closing drawers, all the while muttering under his breath.

Please, please, let him find it, Susie thought as she waited and at last he emerged triumphant from the back room, brandishing a dog-eared card. He tried to smooth it out as he handed it over. 'I don't expect we'll have any more use for it,' he said. 'Good luck with your search.' And with that he disappeared into the back of the shop once more.

Susie murmured her thanks as she left, clutching the tattered card carefully. There was still a possibility that the Bilsons had disposed of all the old records of the family firm so she wasn't out of the woods yet. But it was worth a try. She read the card as she stood outside the building. There was a phone number and an address in Milngavie. She looked at her watch. Did she have time to make the trip there and back before her rendezvous with Alison?

Too bad. She would have to hurry to meet Tony. It would be better to text Alison; say they should get a later train. She could think of an explanation once she'd tracked down any remaining members of the Bilson family.

CHAPTER TWENTY

Tony was sitting at a table in the far corner of the café on the top floor of the John Lewis department store, reading a newspaper. Though she didn't remember ever meeting him, there was a look of her father's family about him, that slightly hooked nose and high forehead. Besides, he stood out as the only man on his own. All the other tables were occupied by little groups of gossiping women or elderly couples, their long association clear by the lack of conversation.

He stood up to greet her. 'Coffee? Or tea?'

Susie shook her head. 'Water would be good.' Tony smiled and hurried over to join the queue.

While she waited for him to return, Susie took the second letter she'd found in the Bible from her bag and reread it. Hopefully Tony could shed some light on this.

He returned, clutching a bottle of water and a glass, smiling as he sat down. 'I must say, Alison, it's great to see you after all these years. You were only so-high when we last met.' He stirred his coffee and coughed. 'But I'm sure there's some special reason for your visit. Well, there must be if you were happy to come all the way out to Culmach on the off chance.'

He raised his eyebrows as he spoke. No point in delaying, thought Susie.

'Yes, there is a reason, or rather several.' Briefly she explained about her inheritance, before ending, 'So you see, I'm trying to find out why the house was left to me, what the family connection was with Robert Fraser. Why on earth would Robert Ainslee have left the house in his care?'

Tony had started to fidget as she told her story and for a moment Susie thought it might be because he thought she had no business contacting him after all this time to quiz him about family history. She stopped talking. 'Sorry, I didn't mean to upset you.' She unscrewed the top of the water bottle and poured some into a glass, waiting for his reply.

He shook his head and smiled. 'No, it's not upsetting. I can help you, but only a little. It was like this, Susie and,' he held up a hand in warning, 'you have to remember times were different, very different. There was a huge family row when your mother married your father. Her family did have wealth at one time - our family had none.' He sighed and closed his eyes, seeming to go off into a reverie and Susie said quickly, 'So mother's family disapproved of my father?'

'What? Oh, yes, very much so. Times were different then and ours was a very poor family from Glasgow, had few prospects, though they were respectable enough. I suppose you might have called them in those days 'rough and ready'. And even when your father died, the rift didn't heal.'

That explained one part of the story, thought Susie but not all of it.

'Okay. I understand how that might happen. But what was the connection with Robert Fraser? How come my aunt and uncle, the Ainslees...' she stopped. 'Sorry, I know now the relationship was more distant than that, but I can only think of them as my aunt and uncle. Why were they living in the lodge and not at Ettrick House? Why was I sent there?'

Tony hesitated. 'I'm not sure how to tell you this, Susie, but the 'aunt' and 'uncle' you spent your holidays with weren't the Ainslees - they were the Frasers. They were the people who lived in the lodge house. You were a relative of Robert Ainslee, but that was the arrangement.'

Susie gasped. She could feel herself saying, as though from a great distance, 'The Frasers? Why was I living with the Frasers?'

Tony nodded. 'I can't believe you were never told of the connection, but I think your stepfather didn't want to become involved in the problems of your mother's family.'

'Hold on. Wait a minute. Explain a bit more.'

'I'm not entirely sure of the details. The connection wasn't that close. Robert Ainslee was a second,' he hesitated and frowned, 'or was it a third cousin? Anyway, he was the only one on your mother's side who felt sorry for her, but not enough to help her openly once your father died.'

'Why not? Surely if he owned Ettrick House he was able to do as he wished?' Now she'd recovered from the initial shock, Susie could feel the anger bubbling up inside her.

Tony shook his head. 'Not quite. He didn't want to be directly responsible. I assume, as he was on his own and given the family's views, he thought this a better way of dealing with the situation.'

'And were Uncle Robert and Aunt Jeanie, sorry I mean the Frasers, also poor relatives he was helping?'

Tony shook his head. 'No, they weren't related in any way. They helped run the estate, at least Robert did.'

Susie put her head in her hands. 'Wait, wait, this is so bizarre. Let me try to understand. My mother was related to Robert Ainslee, but though he wanted to help her, he didn't do so directly. Instead he arranged for me to stay with his employees in the lodge house?'

Tony shrugged. 'That's the way it was. Your mother was probably grateful for any help in the circumstances. By marrying your father, in spite of a lot of opposition, the family believed she'd chosen to cut herself off. And our, your father's, family were in no position to help.'

'Then what about this.' Susie scrambled in her bag and brought out the scrap of a letter she'd found in the Bible and passed it over.

Tony took it carefully and opened it as though expecting something to jump out at him and after glancing at it briefly, handed it back.

Impatient at Tony's attitude, Susie could stand the silence no longer. 'It looks as if it's part of a love letter. I found it in the family bible in the Lodge. Was it Aunt Jeanie's? I know they had no children, suspect they weren't even married. Was she having an AFFAIR?' A thought struck her. 'An affair with Robert Ainslee?'

Tony shook his head. 'Ah, there's the story, Susie. No, that wasn't the case. Oh, Robert Fraser and Jeanie were married all right though, from the family rumours I heard as I was growing up, it was more what you'd call a marriage of convenience.'

'So what about this letter?' Susie began to read aloud,

'My dearest,

Time passes so slowly and I know nothing becomes easier, but have courage. I WILL do something to help you, to make sure…

…leave to you my house, there being no one else to take charge…'

Tony sat in silence as she paused. 'I know it's only a scrap, but it must mean something.'

He took a deep breath, appearing to make a decision.' Look, Susie, I don't know the whole story, but there have been whispers in the family for many years. Mind you, I'm not saying they are more than tittle-tattle, but perhaps this letter makes it seem more likely.' Tony shifted in his seat, turning away as his face became red.

'What are you talking about?' Susie couldn't contain her impatience. 'Are you saying this isn't about the woman I knew as Aunt Jeanie?'

Tony took a deep breath. 'I told you things were different then. It's like this. Robert and Jeanie were married - it was almost essential in those days. But more than that - it was possibly - and I'm only saying possibly - a cover.'

'A cover for what?' Would Tony never get to the point?

'Let's just say the rumour was that the man you thought was your uncle Robert and Robert Ainslee had an association that was more than master and servant. His wife and child had died in childbirth and Robert Ainslee was determined his beloved house wouldn't fall into the wrong hands. He trusted Robert Fraser to do what was right.'

Susie opened her mouth to speak, but no sound came out. Whatever she'd expected, it wasn't this.

Having given this information, Tony appeared anxious to leave as quickly as he could. He stood up, saying abruptly, 'That's as much as I know, Susie. I'm only sorry I can't help you any further.'

'Wait, wait,' said Susie as he started to put on his coat. 'I might want to meet up with you again.'

They exchanged addresses and she said goodbye to Tony with promises to keep in touch, though she doubted if they would do more exchange Christmas cards.

She sat for a moment after he left, trying to take in this latest piece of news. Was it possible that Tony was correct and this Robert Ainslee and Robert Fraser had had a relationship?

She glanced at her watch then jumped up as she realised she'd have to hurry if she was to find time to meet with Percy Bilson before heading back to Bute.

CHAPTER TWENTY-ONE

When Susie phoned, Percy Bilson couldn't disguise his surprise at this contact about his family firm which had been closed for many years and she had to repeat her request several times. She reasoned this was the kind of thing much better done face-to-face and having come so far, encountered so many dead ends, she didn't want to fail at the last hurdle through an unguarded comment. If Percy Bilson couldn't provide a lead she would have to give up her quest.

'Are you sure you have the right person,' he said, his quavery voice betraying his age.

'Absolutely,' replied Susie, 'and I promise I won't take up much of your time.'

At last, in the face of her persistence, he agreed to see her if she could make the trip out to Milngavie. 'You're lucky to have caught me. It so happens I'm just back from a trip to Perth to see my son and his family and I'm having a day or two at home to recover.'

Susie paused for a moment. Perhaps this visit wasn't such a good idea. He must be in a very frail state if a trip to Perth necessitated two days recovery, but when he added, 'It's such a long flight, you know,' she realised he meant Perth, Australia.

'I can be there in an hour,' said Susie, eager not to lose the advantage and hoping Milngavie station had a taxi rank because she had the impression Percy Bilson lived a little way out of the village.

As she hurried up to Queen Street station, wondering about the time of the next train, she passed a line of taxis sitting patiently at the rank and on impulse jumped into the nearest one. Time, not money, was important now.

Luckily the driver was happy to chatter on about the weather, the price of housing and various other topics with little input from Susie and she was able to rehearse what she'd say once she arrived at the Bilsons'.

At this time of day the traffic was light and they made good time to her destination. If the meeting didn't last too long and she could get a taxi back, she might yet make the train she and Alison had agreed on.

As they drove along through Milngavie, she was glad she hadn't trusted to luck. Each house was larger and more imposing than the next and when they turned into Tannoch Road and drew up outside the address she'd been given, she couldn't help but be impressed.

She paid the taxi driver and added a generous tip, all the while looking at the double fronted house of grey stone with the name Loch Haven prominently displayed on a large metal sign at the entrance.

Susie rang the bell and waited, glancing over at the loch which gave the house its name, to watch a mother with a highly excitable toddler who was taking great pleasure in throwing bread to the ducks.

She half expected the door to be opened by a butler, but it was Percy Bilson himself, a small, stooped, desiccated man, who opened the door. He was welcoming, but cautious.

'I'm not sure how I can help you,' he said, ushering her in and inviting her to take a seat in the little room which appeared to serve as a study, judging by the piles of paper on the old-fashioned desk as well as liberally strewn on shelves, tables and even the floor.

'It's a long story about a property I've inherited,' said Susie, thinking she might as well plunge straight in, to which he frowned saying, 'Now you've intrigued me.'

Susie tried to tell the story without wasting too much time, but at several points Percy held up his hand. 'Whoa! Slow down a bit, my dear. I'm finding it hard to take in all these relatives of yours.'

'Sorry, sorry,' said Susie, concerned she might lose his attention.

'So,' a confused look flitted across his face, 'how do you think I can help you with this?'

Susie pulled the crumpled piece of paper from her bag and passed it over. 'I think the Bilson firm dealt with this.'

Percy examined the paper for some minutes, then burst out laughing. 'I'm so sorry, but I really don't think this is of much help.'

'Yes, but,' said Susie leaning forward eagerly, 'you must have records of the firm, details of their dealings.'

Percy shook his head. 'Most of that stuff was done away with ages ago.' He waved his hand expansively. 'I mean, this is a large house, but even here room is limited.'

Susie bit back a comment about space being limited because there was so much paper strewn around. Secretly she'd been wondering how anything could be found among this mess. 'So there's nothing?' Susie sat back, her face registering her disappointment.

'Ah, I didn't say that, not exactly.' He wagged his finger. 'Most of the records were destroyed but some of them were of historical interest and were passed to the archives of the Mitchell Library in Glasgow.'

If he thought this would help, he was mistaken. A trip to the Mitchell Library would involve staying in Glasgow overnight and there was no way she could do that without revealing to Alison what she had been up to. Even then there might be nothing of help in the papers stored in the archives.

Susie stood up. 'I'm sorry to have bothered you. I guess there's no way I can get any further forward.'

Percy Bilson clearly caught her mood of disappointment. There was a pause before he said, 'Wait a minute. I've remembered. There is something that might help. My great grandfather kept a kind of work notebook and he was a very meticulous man. We have those in the house as well as some of his papers. I thought they might be of interest to the children because there's a lot of personal information also. They led a great life in those days.'

He waved his hand to encompass the area. 'This house echoed to the sound of parties and weekend soirees…' His voice trailed off and Susie, anxious to bring him back to the present said, 'And I'd be able to see these notebooks?'

He seemed to recollect himself. 'Eh? I don't see why not. Wait there a minute and I'll try to find the relevant boxes.'

He got slowly to his feet, leaning heavily on his ornate cane and disappeared off, leaving Susie fretting. If she couldn't find what she was looking for quickly, would he trust her to borrow them and examine them at her leisure? Why should he? She was a complete stranger as far as he was concerned, in spite of her story.

Much sooner than she anticipated he came back staggering under the weight of a large cardboard box. Susie rushed to help him and set it down on the only space on the desk that wasn't entirely covered.

'Let's make room,' he said, sweeping a pile of papers off to join the others on the floor. Susie knew she wasn't the most organised of people, but this method of filing left her aghast.

Percy seemed unaware of the effect he had created, opening the box and beginning to rummage through, coughing a little as a cloud of dust rose. After a moment or two, while Susie sat with bated breath, he straightened up, saying, 'This is the one – I'm sure the years you want are in here.'

'Don't think I'm ungrateful,' said Susie biting her lip, 'but I have to get back to Bute this evening. I'm meeting a friend for... Oh, heavens I meant to text her to suggest the later train.'

She whipped out her phone as Percy again began sorting through the box, crossing her fingers that Alison would agree to her request without asking questions.

The reply came zinging back: 'Suits me. Meeting Deborah for tea if we're going for a later ferry.'

As she closed the phone down with a feeling of relief, Susie craned forward to see what Percy had found.

There were a number of notebooks and various papers in the box – undisturbed for a long time by the looks of them, but Percy seemed to be familiar with them.

'Eh, so what was the year you were looking for?'

'I'm not sure,' said Susie, 'I can only suggest we make a guess.'

'Aha,' said Percy brandishing a couple of the notebooks and wiping them with his sleeve. 'These, if I'm not much mistaken, should be what we're after.'

Susie had the distinct impression Percy was very much enjoying this. Perhaps his children weren't as interested in the family history as he'd hoped.

He passed one of them to Susie and she took it with trembling hands. 'You check this one and I'll make a start on this.'

Was the answer in one of these notebooks? Would she at last find out how she had come to inherit the house at Ettrick Bay?

CHAPTER TWENTY-TWO

It took time to get used to the old-fashioned writing, but once she'd become accustomed, Susie was able to make rapid progress through the first notebook.

Mr. Bilson senior had most certainly been an organised man. Each day contained details of everything he'd done both at work and at home; right down to every morsel of food he'd eaten.

'These are a terrific historical treasure trove,' breathed Susie, trying hard not to be distracted from her task as she read on.

Percy smiled. 'Yes, they most certainly are. They'll eventually join the rest of his archive, but not yet. Sometimes of an evening I like to sit in here in the quiet and read some of the entries. It makes me feel as if he's still alive.'

'Oh, gracious.' Susie stopped, her finger poised over one of the entries. 'This looks as if it might be exactly what I'm after.'

She showed the piece of paper, which appeared to be a copy stuck in half-way through the notebook, to Percy.

'Mmm, you could be right. Let's take it over to the table by the window where the light's better.' Now that there was a discovery, Percy appeared to be excited by Susie's find.

They settled by a large table covered with yet more teetering piles and once more Percy sorted them by the simple method of sweeping them all aside to the far end. Percy, thought Susie, wasn't as meticulous as his grandfather.

She ignored the first part, though it was interesting to read that the weather had been as unpredictable then as it was now and began to read aloud from what appeared to be a missive from Robert Ainslee.

'22nd September

Did this day meet again with Mr. Bilson to discuss the disposal of Ainslee House. Having no issue and with Beatrice no longer here, there is nothing I can do to hand on this property at present. Robert Fraser is unhappy about agreeing to the arrangement, but I think I have finally persuaded him it will be for the best. He has no children, but he and his wife have been so kind to my relative, a delightful child who spends all her time here during her school holidays. In spite of the lowly background of her father I wish her to be my heir. I trust Robert to guard her inheritance.'

Susie broke off, feeling herself blush as this description of her and she could hear Percy chuckling, though she didn't dare look round to meet his gaze.

'So?' he said, 'Don't you want to continue?'

Susie took a deep breath.

'When I am gone, which I guess will not be too long from now, I want to know this place will not fall into the wrong hands. I have left also a sum of money for the upkeep of the house. I am placing all my trust in Robert Fraser as a good and trusty friend.'

There was a silence in the room as Susie finished reading.

'Does that answer your question?' Percy asked in a soft voice. 'I expect my grandfather had a copy made as it was such an important decision.'

'Yes, yes,' Susie's mind was still on the details of the bequest and there were questions remaining in spite of this piece of information. For one thing, if Robert Ainslee had left money for the upkeep of the house, where was the money? The people she'd stayed with in the lodge house, the couple she'd thought were her aunt and her uncle, had always struck her as frugal and surely Ainslee would have had some idea of the amount of money needed to maintain a property the size of Ettrick House.

'So the man I knew as my Uncle Robert - he must surely have made a will?'

Percy shrugged. 'I would think that's what Robert Ainslee wanted, but once the property was handed over to Robert Fraser, he would have no control over the matter. Perhaps Mr. Fraser didn't want to become involved with the business of making a will, didn't want too many questions asked.'

There might indeed have been a good reason he didn't bother with a will. If the story about his relationship with Robert Ainslee was true he wouldn't want to draw attention to it, thought Susie. Aloud she said, 'But Inheritors Limited tracked me down.'

'Of course,' said Percy, as though surprised. 'That's what they do.' He chuckled. 'Let's hope a will by Robert Fraser doesn't turn up. You might miss out on your inheritance if he left the property to someone else.' He lifted his hands. 'Only joking.'

Susie's mind was on practical matters. 'Is there any way I can have a copy of this?'

'Take it with you. I'm sure you'll return it in good time. It's only a copy.'

As she stood up to leave, she said, 'But what about the money for the upkeep of Ettrick House? There's no evidence of that, is there?'

Percy chuckled. 'I suspect there wasn't any money, my dear. Poor Robert Fraser was told this so that he would agree to take on the house. The truth is that Ainslee was a bit of a gambler by all accounts. The house was eventually allowed to fall into decay.'

'That's for sure,' said Susie, thinking of the weed choked gardens, the rusting ironwork, the damp and rotting woodwork.

'Mmm, sad, but that's what happened to so many of these large houses.'

'Oh, I see. So that's why the house was so sparsely furnished? Robert Fraser had to sell some of the valuables to make ends meet?'

'Mmm, we can speculate all we like, but yes, that is the most likely scenario, though why he didn't sell the big house, we'll never know.'

Susie made for the door, thanking Percy profusely, impatient to leave as quickly as possible in case he changed his mind about lending her the document.

Once outside, she whipped out her mobile phone to dial for a taxi, before remembering she wasn't far from the station. It would surely be quicker to take the train into town. Besides at this moment what she needed more than anything was time to think.

There might be loose ends to tie up, but she had a better understanding of why she had come to inherit the house at Ettrick Bay. Secrets and lies. Family secrets - so much hidden for so many years.

She still found it hard to believe the people she'd known as Uncle Robert and Aunt Jeanie hadn't been related in any way, had been the custodians of Ettrick House, the property she had been destined to inherit.

It wasn't over, not by a long way. There were decisions to be made about the house. But at least she now knew the truth, though the story of her relations, the Ainslees, was far from over.

It was time to go back to the Isle of Bute, back to Ainslee, or rather, Ettrick House and time to tell Alison everything and seek her help. Whatever happened, this was something she couldn't do alone.

Did Susie sell Ettrick House? Or did she decide to keep her inheritance? The story of her decision is told in The House at Ettrick Bay.

ACKNOWLEDGEMENTS

Grateful thanks to

Joan Fleming, Bill Daly and Judith Duffy for reading and suggestions, Paul Duffy and Rosemary Gemmell for help with technical issues.
And thanks to Peter for his memories of Bute.

THE HOUSE AT ETTRICK BAY

PROLOGUE

At Ettrick Bay, the sun is going down, the rippling light casting long shadows across the water. Along the shore, the oyster catchers gather, shrieking in the gloaming. No boats disturb the tranquillity of the steel grey waters lapping at the shore.

The cattle in the fields beside the long path look up, startled by the sound of plough horses returning home. In the darkening sky, the stars appear one by one as the pale crescent moon casts a ghostly light across the fields ripe with corn.

High above the bay, Ettrick House stands brooding, steadfast in the autumn winds. Couch grass and bindweed choke the once well tended flower beds and the long sweeping drive is pitted and potholed. The windows are shuttered, dark.

Alone in the silence of the empty house he sits nursing a glass of whisky, gazing at the pictures he sees in the flickering flames of the fire set against the chill of the evening.

Now, in his old age, the ghosts come back to haunt him. They give him no rest. And he wonders if tonight will be the night when at last she is found.

.

Lightning Source UK Ltd.
Milton Keynes UK
UKOW04f0640211115

263201UK00002B/8/P